"Where are you?" Heidi whispered. She stepped back outside to scan the parking lot.

A figure walked toward her. She studied him, but it wasn't the man she'd come to meet.

As he got closer, he lifted his gaze and connected with hers. Blue ice chips bored into her.

She whirled to go back into the restaurant, but a hard hand grabbed her ponytail and yanked her toward her car. She let out a scream and threw an elbow back. She connected, and her attacker let out a harsh grunt.

His grip relaxed a fraction, and Heidi lashed out with a foot, connecting with a hard knee. He cried out and went to the asphalt.

And she was free.

* * *

MILITARY K-9 UNIT:
These soldiers track down a serial killer
with the help of their brave canine partners

Lynette Eason is a bestselling, award-winning author who makes her home in South Carolina with her husband and two teenage children. She enjoys traveling, spending time with her family and teaching at various writing conferences around the country. She is a member of Romance Writers of America and American Christian Fiction Writers. Lynette can often be found online interacting with her readers. You can find her at Facebook.com/lynette.eason and on Twitter, @lynetteeason.

EXPLOSIVE FORCE

LYNETTE EASON

◆ **HARLEQUIN**® LOVE INSPIRED® SUSPENSE

Special thanks and acknowledgment are given to Lynette Eason for her contribution to the Military K-9 Unit miniseries.

Recycling programs
for this product may
not exist in your area.

LOVE INSPIRED BOOKS

ISBN-13: 978-1-335-49058-2

Explosive Force

But the Lord is faithful, who shall stablish you,
and keep you from evil.
                        —2 Thessalonians 3:3

Dedicated to the two-legged and four-legged heroes
who put their lives on the line every day.
No amount of thanks will ever be enough.

ONE

First Lieutenant Heidi Jenks, news reporter for *CAF News*, blew a lock of hair out of her eyes and did her best to keep from muttering under her breath about the stories she was being assigned lately.

She didn't mind the series of articles she was doing on the personnel who lived on the base—those were interesting and she was meeting new people. And besides, those had been her idea.

But some of the other stories were just plain boring. Like the stolen medals. Okay, maybe not boring, but definitely not as exciting as some she could be working on. Like finding Boyd Sullivan, the Red Rose Killer. A serial killer, he liked to torment his victims with the gift of a red rose and a note saying he was coming for them. And then he struck, leaving death and heartache in his wake with one last rose and a note tucked under the arm of the victim. *Got you.*

Heidi shut the door to the church where her interviewee had insisted on meeting and walked down the steps, pulling her voice-activated recorder from her pocket. She might as well get her thoughts down before they dissipated due to her complete disinterest. She shivered and glanced over her shoulder. For some reason she expected to see him, as if the fact that she was alone in the dark would automatically mean Sullivan was behind her.

After being chased by law enforcement last week, he'd fallen from a bluff and was thought to be dead. But when his body had never been found, that assumption had changed. He was alive. Somewhere. Possibly injured and in hiding while he healed. Reports had come in that he'd been spotted twice in central Texas. She supposed that was possible. But what if the reports were wrong? What if he'd made his way back here to the base so he could continue his reign of terror?

The thought quickened her steps. She'd feel better behind a locked door where she could concentrate on the story she was currently working on.

Someone on the base was breaking into homes and stealing war medals, jewelry and cash. Whatever small items they could get their hands on. But it was the medals that were being targeted. Medals of Valor especially. People were antsy enough about the whole serial killer thing. Having a thief on base wasn't helping matters.

She spoke into the recorder. "Mrs. Wainwright stated she hadn't been home at the time of the robbery. However, as soon as she pulled into her drive, she could see her open front door and knew something was wrong."

Heidi's steps took her past the base hospital. She was getting ready to turn onto the street that would take her home when a flash of movement from the K-9 training center caught her eye. Her steps slowed, and she heard a door slam.

A figure wearing a dark hoodie bolted down the steps and shot off toward the woods behind the center. He reached up, shoved the hoodie away and yanked something—a ski mask?—off his head, then pulled the hoodie back up. He stuffed the ski mask into his jacket pocket.

Very weird actions that set Heidi's internal and journalistic alarm bells screaming. And while she wanted to see what the guy was going to do, she decided it might be more prudent to get out of sight while she watched.

Just as she moved to do so, the man spun.

And came to an abrupt halt as his eyes locked on hers.

Ice invaded her veins, sending shivers of fear dancing along her nerves. He took a step toward her, then shot a look back at the training center. Back to her. Then at his wristwatch. With no change in his granite ice-blue eyes as he gave her one last threatening glare, he whirled and raced toward the woods once again.

Like he wanted to put as much distance between him and the building as possible.

Foreboding filled her just as a side door to the training center opened. A young man stood there, his uniform identifying him as one of the trainers. His eyes met hers, just like the hooded man's had only seconds earlier. But this time, she knew who the eyes belonged to. Bobby Stevens, a young airman who'd recently finished his tech training. He hesitated, glanced at her, then over his shoulder.

Her gut churned with a distinctly bad feeling. With everything that had happened on the base in the last few months, there was only one reason that the man in the hoodie would be so anxious to run when it looked like he would rather do her bodily harm.

She started backing away, her feet pedaling quickly. "Run, Bobby! Get away from the building. Something weird is going on!"

Bobby hesitated a fraction of a second, then took off

toward her, looking determined to catch up with her. Her footsteps pounded as she put distance between her and the building and the man behind her.

Then an explosion rocked the ground beneath her and she fell to her knees, her palms scraping the concrete as she tried to catch herself.

Rolling, Heidi held on to her screams and looked back to see part of the building missing and fire spurting from the cavernous area.

And Bobby Stevens lying sprawled on the ground.

People spilled from the buildings close to her, many on their phones. No doubt calling for help.

Heidi managed to get her feet beneath her and scrambled to stand. She raced back to Bobby and dropped beside him, wincing as her knees hit the concrete.

Already, she could hear the sirens.

Calling on her past first aid training, Heidi pressed her fingers against his neck and felt a steady, if slow, pulse. He had a laceration on his forehead and his wrist hung at an odd angle.

His lids fluttered, then opened. His brows dipped and he winced.

"It's all right, Bobby," she said. "Help is on the way."

"What happened?"

"The building exploded, but you're going to be okay."

"Exploded? Why?" His eyelids fluttered. "Hurts." He tried to roll and groaned.

Heidi pressed her hands to his shoulders. "I know. Just be still."

"Hold my hand, please," he whispered. "I'm...cold."

She slid her fingers gently around his uninjured hand. "I'm here," she whispered. "Just hold on." Bobby's eyes closed, but he continued to breathe shallow, labored breaths. "You're going to be all right. Just hang in there."

In seconds, she felt hands pulling her away. First responders had arrived. Heidi backed up, keeping her eyes on the now-unconscious man who'd reached out to her as though she could save him.

"Are you all right?" the paramedic asked her.

She focused in on the figure in front of her. "Um… yes. I was farther away from the blast. It knocked me off my feet, but nothing else. I just ran back to check on Bobby."

"Your knees are bleeding."

She blinked and looked down. "Oh." Blood seeped through her slacks. And now that her attention had been brought to them, her knees throbbed.

The paramedic led her to one of the four ambulances now lining the street. "Let me just check you out and get these knees bandaged for you."

"Yes, okay. Thank you." She drew in a deep breath and let her gaze wander past the crowd that had gathered.

Was the bomber watching the building burn? Could he see the firefighters fight against the raging flames?

She had a bad feeling about this. A feeling that this was only the beginning of something that might be bigger than any story she'd ever worked on.

And she had a feeling that the man who'd done this would be back.

Because she'd seen him.

First Lieutenant Nick Donovan itched to get his hands on the person who'd just blown up part of the training center. Thankfully, it was an area of the building that wasn't being used at the moment and no animals had been harmed. Airman Bobby Stevens was reported to be in stable condition and was expected to make a full recovery. That was the only reason Nick's anger wasn't boiling over, even though his patience levels were maxed out.

Unfortunately, he and his bloodhound, Annie, would have to wait a little longer to do their part in figuring out exactly what had caused the explosion. Annie was trained in explosives detection, but right now, she couldn't get near the training center, even wearing the protective booties. The area was still too hot, and firefighters were still fighting the blaze. However, Annie and he *could* examine parts of the building that had landed yards away.

Office of Special Investigations, OSI, had arrived and would be taking lead on the case under the supervision of Ian Steffen. Nick also spotted FBI special agent Oliver Davison, who'd been a frequent visitor to the base—not only because of his search for the Red Rose Killer, but also to see his fiancée, Senior Airman Ava Esposito.

Of course, he would show up. At this point, anything bad that happened on the base was suspected of being caused by Boyd Sullivan. And Oliver was one of the most determined people on the elite investigative team formed especially to hunt Sullivan down and bring him to justice. Truth was, they all wanted the killer caught and were working overtime in order to do that.

Nick belonged to the Explosive Ordnance Disposal unit and had gotten the call shortly after the explosion happened. He'd raced from his home and arrived to find the organized chaos he was now in the middle of. If the EOD unit had been called, then someone thought the damage to the building had been caused by a bomb— and they wanted to make sure there weren't any more explosives waiting to go off. Which he would be happy to do just as soon as he could get close enough.

Security Forces with assault rifles flooded the area and stood ready should there be another attempt to attack, although Nick figured whoever was responsible was long gone. But Canyon Air Force Base had an action plan for this kind of thing and it had been put into place immediately.

From the corner of his eye, he caught sight of Heidi Jenks, one of the base reporters, talking to an OSI investigator.

He scoffed. Boy, she didn't waste a second, did she? He sure hoped the investigator knew how to keep his mouth shut. The last thing they needed was for her to write a story before the facts were even determined.

She ran a hand over her wavy blond hair and rubbed her eyes. He frowned. Where was her ever-present notebook? And why did she look so disheveled?

Annie pulled on the leash and Nick let her lead him over to a large block of concrete. She sat. And he stiffened at her signal, which indicated a bomb. While he didn't think the piece of concrete itself was going to explode, it obviously had explosives residue on it. She looked at him expectantly. "Good girl, Annie, good girl." He took a treat from his pocket and she wolfed it down.

He set his backpack on the ground and pulled out the items he needed to take a sample of the cement. Once that was done, he placed the evidence back in his pack and scratched Annie's ears.

"What was that?" a voice asked. A voice he recognized and sometimes heard in his dreams. Against his will.

He looked up and found himself staring at a pair of bandaged knees. The blood on the torn pants had a story to tell. Nick stood and looked down into Heidi Jenks's blue eyes. Eyes he could drown in if he'd let himself.

But she was so off-limits in the romance department that he banished the thought from his mind as soon as it popped in.

"No comment."

"Come on, Nick."

"Just something I want to take a closer look at."

She turned away to look at the smoking building. Fire trucks still poured water onto it. It could take hours to put the fire out. "It was a bomb, wasn't it?" she said when she turned back to him.

He pursed his lips. "Why do you jump to that conclusion?"

"What else could it be?" She shrugged. "Why else would you and Annie be here along with other members of EOD? You're going to have to check to make sure there aren't any more bombs, aren't you?"

Nick knew Heidi because he'd read her newspaper articles and some of the stories she'd written. Most people would consider them to be fluff pieces, but the truth was, he could see her heart behind them. And whether he wanted to admit it or not, he liked it. He and Heidi had had a few conversations, and each time, he'd wanted to prolong them. Which was weird for him. He didn't do conversations with people like Heidi. Users who just went after the story without worrying about the fallout. Even though his gut told him she wasn't like that. But she had to be. Otherwise he could lose his heart to her. And that couldn't happen. No way.

"Good deductive reasoning," he told her. "But did you think it was possible that I just wanted to see what was going on?"

"No."

"Hmm. You're right. Annie and I'll have to check for more bombs as soon as we get the green light. And that's not confidential so I'm not worried about you saying anything."

She sighed. "Look, I know with all the rumors circulating, no one wants to talk to me, but this...this is different."

An anonymous blogger had been reporting on the Red Rose Killer, his targets and the investigation. Reporting on things that no one but those involved in the investigation could know. Rumor had it that Heidi was the blogger. As a result, she'd been mostly ostracized from anything considered newsworthy when it came to the Red Rose Killer. But Heidi was persistent. He'd give her that.

He nodded to the torn pants and bandaged knees.

"What happened to you?"

She glanced down. "I got knocked off my feet by the blast."

He raised a brow. "You were here?"

"Yes."

Well, that put a new light on things. "Did you see anything?"

"I don't know. Maybe."

"Either you did or you didn't."

A scowl pulled her brows down. "Then I think I did."

"What did you see exactly?"

She drew in a deep breath. "Like I told the OSI agent, I think I may have seen the bomber."

At Nick's indrawn breath and instant flash of concern, Heidi felt slightly justified in her dramatic announcement. She shrugged, not nearly as nonchalant as she hoped she came across. "Honestly, I don't know if he was the bomber or not, but I sure saw someone who looked like he was up to no good. He had on dark clothing and a hoodie—and a ski mask. Why wear a ski mask unless you don't want anyone to know who you are? Anyway, he took that off right before he turned around and looked at me."

"Tell me everything."

As she talked about the man in the hoodie with the ice-cold blue eyes running from the scene, Nick's frown deepened. "You might be fortunate he was in a hurry to get away."

"I think that's a reasonable assumption." Just the thought of him sent fear skittering up her spine.

"So, he knows you saw him."

"Oh, yes, he knows. OSI is rounding up a sketch artist for me to work with." She shivered and crossed her arms at the memory of the man's brief pause, as though he'd considered coming after her. Thankfully, he'd been in a hurry, more worried about getting away from the impending explosion. But she had seen his face. Well, some of it. The hoodie had hidden his hair color and some of his features, but she'd be able to identify those blue eyes anywhere and anytime.

"All right, stick close," Nick said. "I'm going to let Annie keep working and we'll see what she comes up with."

For the next thirty minutes, Heidi did as instructed and stayed right with him. Not just so she could collect facts for the story, but because she was just plain rattled. Okay, scared. She'd admit it. She was afraid and feeling decidedly out of her depth.

But watching Nick and Annie work was a good distraction. She felt safe with Nick in a way she couldn't explain, and she couldn't help admiring his strength and confidence, the total focus and dedication he had to his job.

Her father had been like that.

Before he'd died.

A pang of grief hit her and she shook her head. It had been two years and she still missed him like crazy. But he'd been a wonderful example of the ethical reporter she strived to be. She was determined to follow in his footsteps, determined to make him proud. Thinking of her father naturally sent her thoughts to her mother. A strong woman who'd loved her husband, she'd nearly been shattered by his death. His murder. He'd been killed by the big corporation he'd exposed as a front for the mafia. Killed by his best friend, who'd been the CEO of that corporation.

A lump formed in her throat.

Her parents had argued late one night. She'd come over for dinner and fallen asleep on the couch. When she'd awakened, she'd heard the harsh whispers coming from the kitchen. She'd stayed still and listened, hearing her mother begging her father to stop looking, to "give it up." Her father had been adamant. "I'm not looking the other way, Kate. I can't."

"I'm afraid, Richie," she'd whispered. "I'm truly afraid something will happen to you."

And it had. Not even two weeks later, a jogger had found his body washed up against the shore of a nearby lake. Her father had taken a bullet through the back of his skull. Executed. She lifted her chin. But his work would live on through her. The men who'd killed her father had been captured, tried and imprisoned—including the best friend who'd put the hit out on him. But it didn't bring her father back. It was up to her to carry on his work.

Truth, baby girl. Nothing's more important than exposing lies and bringing truth to light. Keep your focus where it should be. Don't step on people to get to the top. Don't excuse people who do wrong no matter who they are—and you'll do just fine.

Her father's words ringing in her mind, she watched as Nick finally stood from the last place Annie had alerted on and tucked a small bag into the larger one he carried. "All right," he said. "I think I'm done here for now."

"Did you find anything else?"

"I'll have to let the lab decide that." He dug a hand into his front pocket and rewarded Annie with a treat and a "Good job, girl."

His gaze slid to her and he opened his mouth as if to say something, then snapped it shut and gave her a grim smile.

He wasn't going to tell her anything. He didn't trust her. She gave a mental sigh and shrugged off the hurt. What did she expect with everyone thinking she was the anonymous blogger, posting about everything going on in the investigation of the Red Rose Killer? Things no one but the investigative team should know. The blogger had everyone on edge and pointing fingers.

While it was true she was upset she hadn't been assigned the story, that didn't mean she was going around shooting off her mouth about things she shouldn't. The fact was she didn't know anything. Other than what was reported in the papers—and by the anonymous blogger.

But Nick didn't know that. He didn't know *her* other than from a short snippet of conversation here and there. They often ran into each other at the Winged Java café and he always made a point to speak to her—but he kept himself at a distance. Like he didn't want to get too close. For some reason, she wanted to change that.

His eyes narrowed on a spot over her shoulder. She turned to look. "What is it?" she asked.

"I thought I saw something move."

"Everything's moving around here. What are you talking about?"

"In the reserve just beyond the tree line." He strode toward it, Annie on his heels.

Heidi went after him, not about to miss out. Had the guy that set the bomb off stayed behind to watch the action?

But that wouldn't be smart.

Then again, where was the rule that said bombers had to be smart? "You think it could be one of the missing dogs?" she called after him.

Several months ago, after killing two trainers in the Military Working Dog program, Boyd Sullivan had opened all two hundred and seven kennels and released the animals. While the more highly trained dogs had stayed put, one hundred ninety-six dogs, some PTSD therapy dogs—and dogs with PTSD themselves—had escaped. Most had been found and returned to safety, but there were still twenty-one missing.

Nick reached the tree line and stopped, planting his hands on his hips. Heidi caught up and he shook his head. "No, it wasn't a dog. This shadow had two legs."

"Okay. You see him?"

"No." He sighed and rubbed a hand at the back of his neck. "Maybe I'm just imagining things. Like my nerves are so tight it's causing hallucinations."

"But you really don't believe that, so you want to keep looking, right?"

He slid a sideways glance at her. "Yes."

"Then I'm going with you."

"It's probably nothing."

"I'll just tag along and make that decision myself, okay?"

"No, not okay. Stay here."

"The longer you argue with me, the less likely you are to find out if you saw something."

He shot her a black look and turned on his heel to go after whatever it was he thought he saw.

She shrugged and fell into step beside him, doing her best to ignore the pain in her knees. They were going to be sore for a few days, so she might as well get used to it.

Usually Heidi didn't notice how small she was in comparison to the men she worked with on a regular basis, but being next to Nick made her feel positively tiny. And feminine.

Which was stupid. Okay, not necessarily stupid, but seriously—why was she so hyperaware of him? Why did she notice every little thing about him? Like the way his blue eyes crinkled at the corners when he was amused. Or the way his jaw tightened and his lips flattened into a thin line when he was annoyed. Or how his dark hair was never allowed to grow too long. She shouldn't notice those things. But she did.

Nick was no more attracted to her than he was to the tree they'd just walked past, so she really needed to get over whatever it was she felt for him. The last thing she needed was to set herself up for heartbreak.

"I think he went this way," Nick said, pulling her from her thoughts.

She followed even though she didn't see what he did.

The farther they got from the kennel and all of the action, the more she thought he'd seen a bird or something. She hoped so, anyway. The adrenaline crash was coming now that the danger was over. It *was* over, wasn't it? "You see anything else?"

"No. I've lost sight of him."

"So it was definitely a him?"

"Yes."

Before she knew it, they were standing in front of her home. "Wait a minute, he came this way?" she asked.

"Yeah, that's what it looked like."

"This is my house, Nick."

"I'd better check the area. Stay put."

"You keep saying that."

"And you keep ignoring me."

This time she listened and let him do his job. With Annie at his heels, he walked around the left side of her home, then the right, which was next to the home that Staff Sergeant Felicity James shared with her husband, Master Sergeant Westley James. Felicity was still a target of the serial killer, but at least she had her husband to keep an eye out for her. Westley was part of the investigative team looking for Sullivan. A team Heidi really wanted to be a part of.

Nick returned with a frown.

"What is it?" she asked.

"I'm not sure. I thought I saw some footprints in the grassy area along your back fence, but I didn't see anyone."

"I see. That's a bit concerning, but it could be from anyone walking back there, using it as a shortcut."

"I suppose. Could be."

"Okay, well, I'm ready to call it a night," she said.

"I don't blame you. I'll wait here and make sure you get inside safely, then I'll head back to the training center. I don't think Annie and I can do much of anything else, but I'll see if OSI wants us to."

"I've given my statement, so they know where to find me if they have any more questions for me."

"Perfect."

He stood there a moment longer, looking down at her as though hesitant to leave. "Are you going to be all right?" he asked.

"I think so. Why?"

He glanced around one more time. "I don't like that we wound up here while we were following him. He disappeared too easily. Too quickly. If what you say is true, that guy got a good look at you."

"*If* it's true? Really?" She sighed. "I'll be fine, Nick. Good night."

A scuff of a foot just ahead and around the side of her house stopped her.

Nick turned toward the noise. "What was that?" he asked.

"I don't know. Probably nothing." Maybe. Without thinking, she slipped her hand into his.

He squeezed her fingers, then released them. "Stay behind me."

Not quite ready to argue with him, she followed his order as he and Annie led the way. They walked down the sidewalk in front of Heidi's home and were almost to the end of the small property when she saw the shadow skirting around the side of her house. "Hey! Can I help you?" she called.

The shadow took off.

Nick and Annie followed. The fleeing person wove in and out, between the houses, down alleys. Heidi fell back slightly as she realized there was no way she could keep up with Nick's long stride.

She didn't realize he'd stopped until she was almost next to him. Nick had the guy close to being boxed in a corner with no escape. There were buildings on either side of him and an open parking lot too far away from him to flee. He must have realized it the same time she did.

Because he spun and lifted his arm.

"He's got a gun!"

The words were barely out of her mouth before something heavy slammed into her, and she hit the pavement.

TWO

Nick rolled off Heidi and leaped to his feet. He placed himself in front of her as he faced the armed man, disgusted that he'd had no time to pull his own gun—and it was too late to do so now with their attacker's finger on the trigger. "Drop the weapon," Nick ordered.

"Not a chance." The low voice trembled, but Nick couldn't tell if it was from fear or sheer determination not to be caught. The low ball cap and hoodie kept the man's features well hidden. "I'm getting out of here. And if you set that dog on me, she'll take the first bullet. Understand?" He slid sideways, toward the street.

"What are you doing here?" Heidi asked. "Did you blow up the training center?"

But the man wasn't interested in answering, just escaping past Nick. And as long as the man held a gun on him and Heidi, Nick wasn't moving. Also, with the threat against Annie, it was clear the man knew how dogs and their handlers worked. Nick wouldn't knowingly send Annie after him only to have the guy keep good on his threat to shoot her.

Two more steps brought the man to the edge of Heidi's house. He darted past Nick and Annie, his feet pounding on the sidewalk as he headed toward the parking lot. Nick pulled Heidi to her feet. "Are you okay?"

"Yes. I think that's the same guy I saw run from the training center. I couldn't see his face thanks to the hat and hoodie, but it looks like the same one my guy was wearing."

"Stay here. I'm going after him." He left Heidi as he turned and took up the chase once more. He followed on the man's heels. They would soon be at the fence on the other side of the lot and the guy would have nowhere to go.

But he was also armed.

Nick reported his whereabouts into the radio on his shoulder, requesting backup as he pounded the asphalt in pursuit. Heidi stayed behind him, yelling details to the Military Police dispatch.

Was this guy the bomber? Had he been hanging around to watch the chaos his explosion had caused? To gloat? Or was this someone else altogether?

Determined to catch him, Nick pushed himself harder. Annie stayed right with him, lunging at the end of the leash.

The guy disappeared around the building that backed up to the fence.

Nick followed, rounded the building...

And the guy was gone.

Nick skidded to a stop, slightly winded, but he would have gone a little farther if he could have seen who he was chasing. A piece of cloth on a bush caught his attention. He noted it, his eyes darting, looking for any sign someone might have a gun trained on him, while chills danced up his spine.

Footsteps sounded behind him. He whirled, weapon ready. Only to come face-to-face with Heidi. She flinched and he lowered his gun. "Sorry." Nick spun back to the area where he'd lost the suspect. Annie whined and shifted. "What is it, girl?"

Annie looked up at him, her soft, sad eyes asking permission. He glanced at Heidi. "Keep your eyes and ears open, will you? Let me know if anything catches your attention."

She nodded.

Nick slipped his weapon back into the holster and pulled a pair of gloves from the bag on his shoulder. He snapped them on, then reached for the piece of cloth and studied it. Had this been snagged recently? Or had it been there awhile? It didn't look like it had weathered much. He held it out to the dog. "Annie, seek." She sniffed, lowered her nose to the ground, then lifted it to check the air.

"She can track, too?" Heidi asked.

"Sure. It's the same concept, and she's a smart dog. You can hardly train a bloodhound to sit, but tracking is so natural for them, the only training needed is for the handler." A slight exaggeration, but not much. He followed the dog cautiously while he spoke, scanning the area. His radio alerted him to backup closing in behind them and on both sides. The base had been shut down and security was tight. There was no way anyone would be able to get off or on the base for now.

But if whoever had been loitering around Heidi's house lived on the base, Annie would find him.

Annie padded her way to the fence at the far side of the parking lot and sat, looking back over her shoulder at him.

Nick squatted next to the animal and eyed the heavy-duty chain-link fence. "It's been cut." He sighed in disgust at the large opening. "This was his way out. He came prepared. He knew exactly where he was going."

"But where was he hiding? You checked my house."

"I'm guessing he jumped the fence into your backyard when he heard me coming. Once Annie and I left, he simply hauled himself back over."

"My backyard? Nice." She grimaced. "But why would he wait so long to leave the base after setting off the explosion?" she asked. "He should have been long gone by now. Why would he be so stupid as to hang around and take a chance on being caught?"

He glanced at her and shook his head. He had his theories on that, but would keep them to himself for the moment.

"You said he knew his way around the base," she said. "That he was familiar with it. I would agree with that. So, why go this way? Why not simply run back to his home?"

"I said he was familiar with it. Doesn't mean he lives on it."

"True."

"Plus think about it…"

"What?" she asked.

"The dogs."

She raised a brow. "Of course. The base is full of them. He figured a dog like Annie could track him. If he left through the fence and had a car waiting…"

"Exactly. There might be some security footage, but since he kept his face covered, that won't help much."

"He took his mask off right before he turned and spotted me," Heidi said. "But even with the hoodie covering part of his features, I'd still be able to pick him out of a lineup. The guy you just chased? I don't know." She sighed. "Think your forensic people could find some prints or something?"

"On what?"

She shrugged. "I don't know. The fence maybe?"

"He had on gloves, I think." He tucked the piece of cloth into an evidence bag. "They'll try, but I'm not holding my breath." He stood.

His frown deepened and he remembered whom he was talking to. "This better not show up on the front page tomorrow."

Heidi stiffened and her lips turned down. "It's a story, Nick."

"And we don't have the facts yet so don't go printing that we chased the bomber. We don't know who we chased."

"I never said he was the bomber. But I *do* know we chased a guy with a gun."

"Heidi…" He sighed and pinched the bridge of his nose.

Backup arrived then, cutting him off, but he held her gaze for a moment longer before turning his attention to the OSI investigators clamoring for answers.

Standing back from the fence so she didn't trample any evidence, but close enough to watch the action, Heidi drew in a deep breath and tried to calm her nerves. She was glad Nick's attention was off her for the moment, but it did little to calm her.

She'd nearly been killed in an explosion, and someone had been lurking at her house and then held her at gunpoint—all in one night.

She ran a hand over her ponytail, hoping she'd hidden how shaken she'd been, how frightened. Pushing the residual fear aside, she pulled her voice-activated recorder from her pocket and hit Play. Holding the device to her ear, she heard herself call out to Bobby, then the explosion, the aftermath, Bobby begging her to hold his hand, her reassurances.

A tear slipped down her cheek and she sent up a silent prayer for the young man. She'd make her notes, then turn the recording over to OSI.

"Heidi?"

She stiffened at the sound of John Robinson's voice. Great. Of course *he* would show up. And of course, even in the midst of all of the chaos surrounding her, he would hone in on her like Annie on a bomb. No offense to Annie. She grimaced, then smoothed her features before turning to face her nemesis. John, the lead reporter for the Red Rose Killer case—and the bane of her existence at the moment—hurried toward her. She couldn't seem to escape the man.

"What are you doing here?" he asked. "You're supposed to be covering the break-ins and medal thefts."

"I am, John. I was on my way home when…things happened. What are you doing here?"

"Looking for you." He pulled out a pad and paper. "What *did* happen?"

Oh, no. No way was she letting him steal this story from her. "John, you're covering the Red Rose Killer, not everything else."

"I'm covering anything that could be related to him. I heard a couple of MPs speculating that Sullivan was back on base and causing trouble. So, see? This is my story. So…give me details."

"I'm still sorting it all out." She shoved a stray hair from her face. "I'm heading home. I'll see you tomorrow sometime."

"Heidi—"

She waved and started walking away from him.

"What's the rush?" he called. "You got to go get your blog post ready?"

Heidi froze, did a one-eighty and marched back to the man who'd been a thorn in her side from the day he stepped onto the base and into the newspaper office. She stopped in front of him, ignoring the stares from those who'd heard his comment. "Once and for all, John Robinson, I am *not* the anonymous blogger. So stop spreading that lie before I sue you for slander."

A hand curled around her right fist. A fist she didn't even remember making. Looking sideways, she found Nick beside her.

"He's not worth it," he said softly.

Drawing in a deep breath, she made a conscious effort to push down her anger. Nick was right. If she punched John, her career would be over. And she'd worked too hard to let him provoke her into losing everything. But she would *not* let him stand there and accuse her of being the anonymous blogger who was plaguing the investigation.

She pulled her hand from Nick's, and leaving John with his jaw hanging, she executed another about-face and headed toward her house. She was tired. Beat, actually. So exhausted it was all she could do to put one foot in front of the other. Not even the adrenaline sputter from the confrontation with Robinson did much to help her energy level.

Once she reached her home, she slipped the key in the lock, opened the door, and stepped inside.

Peace washed over her as she shut the door behind her. She drew in a deep breath and let the atmosphere calm her. Heidi loved her home. It may look boring and ordinary from the outside, but the inside was all her.

Blues and tans, with a splash of orange here and there, her home allowed her to breathe and cast off the worries of the day.

Except she couldn't stop thinking about Bobby and wondering if he had known the man who'd run from the training center only moments before it had exploded. Or was Bobby just an innocent caught up in a dangerous incident?

A knock on the door sent her temper spiraling.

She yanked it open. "I told you—" She snapped her mouth shut when she saw Nick standing there with Annie at his side. "Oh. I thought you were someone else."

"Robinson?"

"What makes you think that?"

A corner of his mouth tilted up. "Sarcasm looks cute on you."

This time it was her jaw that hung.

"Can I come in?" he asked.

She closed her mouth. "Of course." Stepping back, she let them enter, then shut the door. "Den is to your left."

"Thanks. Your place is similar to mine. Smaller, of course." Base housing for those who didn't live with family members was small. Hers was a one-bedroom residence, but at least she didn't have to do the dorm-style living other airmen were stuck with. "But it sure is nicer than mine. It's…calm and soothing. I like it."

"Thanks. That's what I was going for when I picked out the colors. The days around here can be so long and hectic that I wanted something that reminded me of the ocean. Peace and calm."

He settled on her tan couch and Annie curled up at his feet. "Are you all right?"

"I'm—" She stopped. "I was going to say 'I'm fine,' but I'm not sure that's true. I'm actually stressed and annoyed beyond everything with John Robinson. That man pushes me to the very edge." She shot him a look through her lashes. "Just in case you didn't pick up on that."

"I think I might have."

"Thank you, by the way, for keeping me from slugging him. I don't think I would have, even as much as I wanted to, but I can't say for sure that I would have walked away had you not been there."

"I don't think anyone would have blamed you, but yeah. You're welcome."

"I'll also admit I'm shaken from the explosion and the possibility of being shot, but mostly, I'm extremely tired of everyone thinking I'm the anonymous blogger." She let the last word out on a huff and sank into the recliner opposite the couch. At his startled expression, she wished she could retract the words, but it was too late now.

"And you're not? The anonymous blogger, I mean?"

She didn't have the energy to do more than scowl at him. "No, I'm not. I wouldn't do that. And besides, I don't even have the facts that are being reported in the blog. Every time I read it, I learn something new." She laughed. "That blogger is someone who has access to information I only wish I did."

His eyes searched hers and he gave a slow nod. "I think I believe you."

She wilted. "Really? You think?"

"Yes."

"Well…thanks. I *think*." She sighed. "If you believe me, do you have any thoughts on who it *could* be?"

"No."

"Not that you would tell me, anyway, right?"

He raised a brow. "I knew Boyd from basic training, but I didn't have much contact with him. I don't know who he hung out with other than what we've managed to dig up during the investigation—and, of course, the victims."

"That's probably a good thing. Not knowing him too well, I mean. You don't want to be on his radar."

"No kidding. So…" He cleared his throat. "Now that we're away from all the craziness, would you tell me one more time what you saw tonight?"

Gathering her strength, she nodded. "I can tell you, but you can also listen to it."

"What do you mean?"

"My voice-activated recorder picked up most everything. I mean, the guy who ran out of the training center didn't say anything, but—" She stood. "Hold on and let me get my laptop. I'll start transcribing while you listen."

"You recorded it?"

"Not on purpose. I was walking and talking into it when I spotted the trainer coming out of the building. And then the explosion…" She waved a hand. "Just listen."

She brought up a blank document on her laptop, then hit the play button on the recorder. He listened while she typed as fast as her fingers could fly. If she missed something, she could always go back and fix it.

When the sound of the explosion came through, Nick flinched and rubbed a hand over his chin. He listened to her comfort Bobby. The screams of the sirens. He listened to it all. When it ended, he hit the stop button.

Since there wasn't a whole lot of conversation, Heidi was able to get the whole thing transcribed in one listen.

She'd go back and add in her memories and perceptions later for the article. For now, she'd just lived through one of the scariest nights she'd ever experienced, and she was on the edge emotionally.

To put it simply, she wanted Nick to leave so she could crawl into her bed and hibernate until morning. And maybe cry a little. But instead of sending him on his way, she fell silent, not exactly sure that she really wanted to be alone after all. A knock sounded on the door. "Excuse me."

She rose, and he followed her. At her raised eyebrow, he frowned. "Can't be too careful."

Heidi peered out the side window. "Who is it?" she called out.

"Carl Trees. I'm the sketch artist," the man on the porch stated.

"I know him," Nick said. "He's legit."

Heidi opened the door. "Hi. Come on in." The two men greeted one another, and Heidi led them to the kitchen. "Have a seat at the table. Would you like some coffee or a bottle of water?"

"No, thanks. I'm sure you're tired and ready for this day to be over with."

Carl was right about that. She sat next to him and he turned the laptop so she could see it. "All right," he said, "start with the shape of his face."

For the next hour, they worked on the sketch with Heidi doing her best to get the face as detailed as possible. Finally, she sat back and rubbed her eyes.

"That's him?" Nick asked. He stood behind Carl, looking down at the final rendering.

She studied the image on the screen. "As close as I can remember." The icy blue eyes stared back at her from the screen. "The eyes are spot-on, I know that."

Carl had added a hoodie to the man's head, and Heidi shivered. "That's him."

Carl nodded. "Good job. Your descriptions helped a lot."

"Must be the way with words she has," Nick murmured.

"Must be." Carl shut his laptop and rose. "I'll get out of here and get this sent to the powers that be." He looked at Heidi. "If they catch him, they'll want you to point the finger at him."

"I know." She led him to the door. "Thanks for coming over here."

"Not a problem. Have a good night." Carl left, and Heidi shut the door behind him.

Nick placed his hands on her shoulders and turned her to face him. "I'm really concerned," he said.

"About what?"

"You. I think it's important to know whether the guy we chased was the same guy you just described to Carl."

She frowned. "I know. I think it was, but I'm not a hundred percent sure. There was a hoodie involved both times and it looked like the same one. The first time, I locked eyes with the guy running from the training center. They were blue and looked like they'd be right at home in the frozen tundra. The guy at my house had the hoodie pulled low and he kept his head down. I didn't see his eyes, so..." She shrugged and sighed.

"He might not know that. Or think that. I think the man you saw at the training center and the man who pulled the gun on us are one and the same. That's probably why he was here. Waiting on you. The fact that I was with you threw him off, and he decided he'd better retreat."

She grimaced. "I know. I've already thought of that."

A shiver swept through her. She'd planned on a relaxing evening and an early bedtime. Now she wondered if she'd be able to shut her eyes.

Nick could tell his words had worried her in spite of the fact that she'd already put two and two together. He almost felt bad about saying something and confirming her fears. Almost. But she needed to be on the alert.

He'd been standing outside her home for the last twenty minutes, debating what he should do. He simply didn't feel right leaving her. Then again, she did live on a military base. If she needed help, all she had to do was holler.

But what if she couldn't?

He pulled his phone from his pocket and let his finger hover over Master Sergeant Westley James's number. After all, the man and his wife, Felicity, lived next door to Heidi. Surely, he could keep an eye on her. Still, Nick hesitated. He hated to bother him when he had his hands full with the investigation. Then again, it made sense. The man was right next door. Instead of dialing, he pocketed the phone and walked over to Westley's and knocked.

The curtain in the right window opened and Felicity peered at him. She disappeared and the door opened. "Hi, Nick."

"Hey." She wore loose-fitting jeans and a T-shirt that was probably left over from her days as a trainer. Now she spent her time behind the lens of a camera as the base photographer. The change seemed to agree with her. "Is Westley here?"

"I'm sorry, he's not. You want to come in?"

Nick shook his head. "That's all right. I'm concerned

about Heidi and wanted to see if he'd be willing to keep an eye on her place tonight."

Felicity frowned. "I'm sure he would, but there's no telling when he'll be back. What's going on with Heidi?"

"We're pretty sure she saw the guy who blew up the training center and that he knows it."

Felicity's eyes widened. "No kidding. Well, I can understand why you want to take precautions. I'm sorry Westley isn't available to help."

"It's all right. I have one more option."

"Who?"

"Caleb Streeter."

She smiled. "He's a good option. And I'll be sure to keep an eye out as well. And so will Westley when he gets home."

"Thanks, Felicity." She shut the door and Nick dialed Caleb's number as he walked back over to Heidi's home. He stood at the base of her porch steps while the phone rang. Nick had just started to get to know the master sergeant who was now running the K-9 training center. He'd spotted him earlier in the midst of all of the chaos at the explosion site, but hadn't had a chance to say anything as he'd been swamped answering OSI's questions.

"Hello?" Caleb croaked.

"You awake?"

"I'd just dropped off. What's up, Nick?"

"I was going to ask if you'd help me out by keeping an eye on a friend's place for few hours tonight."

"Normally, I'd say yes, but I've got to get a few hours of sleep. I've got to be up and at the training center early to start assessing the damage and filling out insurance paperwork."

"How many hours do you need?"

A sigh filtered to him. "At least five. Only had three last night."

"When's your next day off?"

"It was supposed to be tomorrow."

Ouch. He was asking a lot of his friend, but everyone else he could think of was busy. "Okay, I'll take first shift. You get your five hours, then come over here. I'll buy you a steak dinner." He noticed Annie's ears perking up at the word *steak* and smiled.

"For two," Caleb said. "I'm taking Paisley with me." Paisley Strange was the girl Caleb was trying to get to know—and impress.

Nick rolled his eyes. "Fine. For two." He gave him the address and Caleb hung up. He noticed Felicity had come back outside and was sitting on the steps. He jogged over. "Hey."

"Hey. Is Caleb able to help you out?"

"Yes. For now."

She nodded. "Westley's still working. He called and said he was going to be at the office for a while." She sniffed. "Still smells smoky out here."

"It comes in waves depending on the wind. I'm just going to hang around and keep an eye on things for a few hours. Do you mind if I use your rocker?"

"Make yourself comfortable." She stood. "This Red Rose Killer is about make Westley pull out what little hair he has."

"He's not alone."

She grimaced. "I don't understand how Boyd Sullivan can just disappear, show up to create havoc, then disappear again without a trace. It's ridiculous." Her lips tightened.

Nick grimaced. "And a bit embarrassing." He frowned. "The fact that we haven't caught him just confirms some of the conclusions we've come to. He's got help on the inside." He was fine discussing the case with Felicity as he knew she was privy to the information.

"I agree. But still, you would think he would have tripped himself up by now—or someone would have spotted him and turned him in."

"Even if someone spotted him, how would they know? He seems to be a master at disguises. Not to mention the fact that he'll kill to get the uniform he needs. He's smart and he's extremely careful."

"I remember Westley saying that Sullivan doesn't make a move unless he's sure he won't get caught."

"True." He frowned. "But we're not giving up. He *will* get careless and we *will* get him eventually."

"I know. That's what Westley says, too." She offered him a small smile. "Take care of Heidi."

"That's the plan."

"I'll watch out for her, too. Let me know if I can do anything."

"Could I get a bowl of water for Annie? I've got food with me."

"Sure. And a bottle for you?"

"That would be perfect. Thanks."

Once he and Annie had their water, Felicity slipped inside and Nick turned the porch light off. He took a seat in the wooden rocker.

After a long drink, Annie settled at his feet.

Time passed while Nick did as much work as he could using his iPhone. He requested one of the OSI investigators to stop by so he could give him the evidence he and Annie had collected from the bomb site. The investigator would make sure it was delivered to the lab for examination.

Once he had everything finished that he'd needed to

do related to the explosion, Nick leaned his head back against the rocker and let his gaze linger on Heidi's home. She'd affected him in a big way. Those eyes of hers had brought forth emotions he'd thought he'd locked securely away a little over three years ago after Lillian Peterson had taken his heart and stomped all over it.

But with one outburst laden with frustration and truth, Heidi had snapped the lock like a toothpick. His heart had reacted and that scared him. He could face down guns and explosives, but a woman who had the potential to hurt him? No way. Normally, he'd run as far and as fast as possible. But he couldn't do that with Heidi. She might be in danger, and Nick simply couldn't bring himself to ignore that and abandon her when he could help.

So now he was completely unsettled.

The streetlamp illuminated a figure heading toward them, soft footsteps falling on the sidewalk. Annie sat up, ears twitching toward the noise. Nick focused on the shadow in the darkness, his hand sliding to his weapon. "Who's there?"

The figure stopped. "Nick? What are you doing out here?"

Isaac Goddard? Nick relaxed. The man was a senior airman and turning into a good friend. "Hey, keeping an eye on Heidi Jenks. She's mixed up in everything that went down here tonight."

"I heard about that." Isaac walked over and leaned against the railing. "Glad no one was seriously hurt."

"Bobby Stevens ended up in the hospital but will heal. What are you doing out here?"

"Just walking. I couldn't sleep."

"Nightmares?" Isaac never talked about it, but Nick

knew the man's PTSD, brought on after serving and being wounded in Afghanistan, kept him up most nights.

"Yeah."

"I'm sorry. Any word on Beacon?" Beacon was the German shepherd who'd been in Afghanistan the same time Isaac had been serving and had saved Isaac's life. Now Isaac was determined to bring him home. Unfortunately, red tape and bureaucratic nonsense had delayed that to the point where Isaac was ready to head back to the desert of his nightmares and find the dog himself.

"They found him," Isaac said.

"Wait, what?" Nick sat straighter. "They did? That's great."

"Yes and no. He was found injured and they're not sure he's going to make it."

Nick's hope for his friend deflated. "Oh, no. I'm sorry."

"I am, too. So right now, it's just wait and see." He shook his head. "I can't give up on him, Nick. He's as much military as I am. I was lying there, injured and bleeding, and he came up and settled down beside me. Like he was trying to let me know I wasn't alone."

Nick had heard the story before, but he let Isaac talk. It seemed to help him.

"He stayed right with me," Isaac said. "For hours until my unit buddies were able to get to me and pull me to safety."

"He's a hero, too."

"Exactly." Isaac sighed and rubbed a hand over his face. "Anyway, sorry. Didn't mean to talk your ear off. I'm going to keep walking. Maybe head over to the gym and work some of this energy off."

"Keep the faith, man."

"I'm trying. You keep it for me, too."

"You got it."

Nick watched his friend walk away and sent up a silent prayer for him.

Hours later, when Caleb arrived, Nick was still praying. About a lot of things. But mostly that the night would continue to be as quiet as it had been up to that point.

Caleb yawned and rubbed his eyes. "I'm going to enjoy that steak dinner. I hope this is worth it for you."

Nick looked back over at Heidi's dark home. "It's worth it," he said softly. "Every single penny."

THREE

Thankfully, the night had passed without incident. After pacing for a couple of hours, Heidi had finally checked the locks four times, glanced out the window to see her street quiet and motionless, and fallen into bed. To her surprise, she'd slept well and five hours later awakened with a new sense of purpose.

Before allowing herself to sleep, though, she'd worked on the story of the training center explosion and sent it off to her editor. The man was thrilled with the piece if his email this morning was anything to go by.

The fact that she could have been killed didn't seem to faze him. His "You're okay, right?" tacked on at the end of his gleeful thanks for a firsthand account of the incident seemed to be perfunctory. She imagined him scrolling through her story while asking that, his brain not even registering her response.

It was okay. She didn't need him to care about her, she just needed him to recognize her work. When he'd given the Red Rose Killer story to John Robinson, she'd nearly had a coronary. But she was a good reporter and one day someone would notice that.

One day. As long as she kept working hard and proving herself. And she supposed she could start by figuring out who'd bombed the training center.

To do that, the first order of business was to visit Bobby Stevens in the hospital. Not only did she want to check on him, she'd admit she wanted to get his story. Having him tell his experience at the training center would make for a good story, ending with him being caught in the explosion at the training center. If she approached it that way, her questions wouldn't seem so intrusive or odd—or look like she was working on the Red Rose Killer story.

When she looked at her phone, she found a text from Nick that he'd sent after she'd gone to bed. Caleb Streeter is watching your house. Don't be alarmed if you see him parked across the street. Touched that he'd arranged protection for her, she texted him back. Thanks. Appreciate it.

She called the hospital and learned Bobby was able to talk in between periods of sleep. She hoped to catch him awake.

When she stepped out of her home, she stood for a moment on her front porch. The air still had a smoky scent to it and she shivered even though it promised to be a hot September day.

She glanced around looking for any indication the man from yesterday might be hanging around, but the only person she saw was sitting in a car opposite her home. Caleb. He lifted a hand in a short salute. She returned it and walked over to him. "Thank you for staying out here. You didn't have to do that."

He shrugged. "There's some scary business going down on this base lately. I'm happy to put in a few hours making sure nothing else happens."

"Well, I appreciate it."

"Where are you headed?"

"To the hospital. Thanks again and see you later."

"Sure thing." He took off, his headlights disappearing around the first turn.

Heidi couldn't help sweeping the area once more with her eyes. When nothing alarmed her, she climbed into her car and pulled away from the curb. It wasn't far to the base hospital, but she blasted her air-conditioning. The last thing she needed was to arrive with sweat pouring from her.

Minutes later, she pulled into the parking lot and made her way toward Bobby's room, only to see First Lieutenant Vanessa Gomez near the nurses' station. The petite and attractive critical-care nurse had her dark hair pulled back into a ponytail and was focused on something on her laptop. Heidi walked over and smiled. "Hi."

Vanessa looked up. "Hi, yourself. I read about the explosion in the paper this morning." She frowned. "You were there and wrote the article as well? All last night?"

"Sleep was hard to come by, so I had nothing better to do. I sent it to my editor in time to be printed this morning."

"And you weren't hurt in the blast?"

"I had a scare and got a couple of scraped knees in addition to a few other bruises, but I'm fine. Much better than poor Bobby Stevens. He got the brunt of it, I think."

"At least he's alive."

"There is that." She paused. "Do you mind if I ask you a question about Boyd Sullivan?"

Vanessa's gaze grew hooded. "Depends on what you want to know."

"Just what you thought of him."

"You want to know what I think about a serial killer?"

Heidi wrinkled her nose. "Okay, so maybe I didn't phrase the question right. How do you know him? Why did he target you?"

"Now, that is a question I'd like the answer to myself." She sighed. "I met him one night when he got into a fight. He didn't want to go to the hospital and risk having his superiors find out about it so he asked me if I'd help him. I had a kit in my car and treated him. I was nice to him. He was nice to me. That was it. Or so I thought until I received a note and a red rose. I have no idea why he targeted me or what I did to make him mad." She shuddered and looked around. "But I feel safe here at the hospital. I'm always around people and I take precautions coming and going."

"How scary."

"Yes." Vanessa's gaze slid to the elevator. "Excuse me, I need to grab something from the cafeteria. It's going to be a while before I'll have a chance to eat again."

"Of course. Be careful."

Vanessa shot her a tight smile. "Always."

Once Vanessa was gone, Heidi found Bobby's room number and knocked. When she heard a faint "Come in," she stepped inside to find Bobby sitting up and eating a bowl of Jell-O while a game show played on the television opposite the bed. The remains of scrambled eggs and bacon sat on the plate in front of him.

"Hi, Bobby."

He set his spoon on the tray. "Hey, Heidi." He sounded surprised to see her.

The right side of his face sported a white bandage from temple to chin and his right arm had a cast from elbow to wrist. Other than that, he looked unharmed. "How are you feeling?"

"I have a headache and some other bumps and bruises, but overall, I'd say I'm a very fortunate guy." His eyes narrowed. "You were there. I remember seeing you."

"Yes. I saw the guy come out of the building."

Fear flashed in his eyes. "You yelled at me to run. How did you know it was going to explode?"

"I didn't. I just... I don't know." She shrugged. "Something felt off. This guy came out wearing a ski mask and I figured that meant he was up to no good. He didn't see me at first and took his mask off. When he realized I was there, he was furious, but the way he looked back at the building and decided to run... I really can't explain it."

"When the explosion happened, it knocked me off my feet," he said. "My whole body vibrated with pain—" He reached up and touched the bandage on his head. "You held my hand."

"You asked me to."

He nodded, then winced. "I've got to remember not to move my head." His expression softened. "Thank you for staying with me. I— uh—admit that I didn't want to be alone."

"I understand. I'm glad I could be there for you." She paused. "What else do you remember?"

It was like someone flipped a switch. His open, unguarded expression instantly shut down. "Nothing much."

He was lying.

"Come on, there has to be something."

"Nope. Just coming out of the building and you yelling at me."

"That part of the building is closed. What were you doing in there?"

He flushed. "I often walk through, checking to make sure everything is secure."

"I see." She paused and he started to pleat the sheet. "So, you have cause to believe something's going on in there that needs your attention?"

"What? No, of course not." He frowned at her. "It's just routine, okay? I do it on a daily basis." He shrugged. "It's quiet in there. Gives me a few minutes to clear my head and just take a break, you know?"

"So that's it?"

"Yeah. That's it."

He reached for the remote, so Heidi switched tactics. She had time to take it slow and pull as much information as she could out of him. In his time. She could be tenacious, but she had to be smart, too. There was more than one way to get an answer from someone. Most guys his age had an ego. "You know, people are going to think you're a hero."

"What? How do you mean?"

"I mean, you've been pretty brave through this whole thing. People might even believe you got hurt trying to stop the guy from blowing the center up."

"But I...well...really?"

"Sure."

"Oh."

"And they're going to want to know how you're doing."

He blinked and some of his chilly facade thawed. "Um. Okay. I guess." His curiosity seemed to take over. "How does this work?"

"I just ask you some questions and you answer. Then I run the article by you and if you approve it, I send it to my editor."

"And if I don't like something in it?"

"We change it so you do like it. I won't print it if you don't approve."

"I see." He thought for a moment. "What kind of questions."

"Questions like…" She looked at the game show he was watching on the television. "How good are you at solving those puzzles?"

His brows shot up and he smiled. "Not very good. I used to watch this show with my mother all the time. She's brilliant and can figure them out with the least amount of letters." He paused. "It's quite frustrating to play against her, actually. But fun, too. I always try to beat her and rarely can do it."

"Sounds like a good mom."

"The best."

"Is she coming to visit?"

He started to shake his head and then paused. "No. It's too far for her. She's in a wheelchair, with MS."

"Oh, I'm sorry."

A shrug. "Been that way my whole life, but didn't stop her from being a great mom. She's already called me several times and I know she'd be here if she could."

"I'm sure she would." Heidi nodded to the television. "Want to watch while we talk?"

Frowning, he tilted his head, then shrugged. "Sure."

Heidi nodded at the television. "Can you solve that one?"

He laughed. "No."

Caleb's phone call informing him that Heidi was leaving her home spurred Nick to action. "Where'd she go?"

"She said she was headed to the hospital. I can't follow her. I have to get over to the training center ASAP."

Hospital? Why?

The trainer who was hurt in the blast. She was going to question him. "Fine. Thanks for your help last night. Let me know when you're planning on that steak dinner."

"Will do."

Nick's next call was to Master Sergeant Westley James. He let the man know he was heading out to find Heidi, who was a possible witness to the bombing.

"Before you go, have you seen the paper this morning?" Westley asked.

"No, I haven't had the time." His gut clenched. What had Heidi done?

"There's a story on the bombing. Heidi Jenks wrote it."

"And?"

A pause. "The story is actually good. Facts and no opinions. Good reporting," he said with a faint smile in his voice, "in my opinion."

Nick paused. Wow. "Um…good to hear that." And a huge relief. "She said that's all she would write. She kept her promise."

Westley huffed. "I've known Heidi for a while now. At first, I was skeptical of her, but since I moved into Felicity's place next door to her I've gotten a different perspective. She seems to be a good reporter who keeps her word. It's impressive. I'll have to admit that before getting to know her, I never would have believed it possible."

"You're not the only one."

"She's also started doing those personality pieces on enlisted personnel. I've read them and they're good. I've even learned a few interesting tidbits about the people I work with. It's nice."

"I'm glad to hear that." And he was. But he needed to get going if he was going to catch up to Heidi.

"Might change my mind and let her do one on me," Westley said.

"She asked?"

"Yes, but I said no at the time." He hesitated, then said, "She's a reporter, after all."

"Yes, she sure is."

To Nick's relief, the man made a sound like he was getting ready to wrap up the conversation. "All right. I know you're working with the investigative team on this Red Rose Killer case. I was talking to Justin and he said OSI wants you on the bombing as well. The evidence you and Annie found has been sent off and we're waiting to hear back. Until then, you might want to keep Heidi in your sights. If we've got a bomber out there who thinks she knows something, she could be in danger."

"Exactly." Which was why he needed to get moving.

"All right. Stay in touch and keep me updated, if you don't mind."

"Of course."

He hung up and whistled for Annie. She came running and stood impatiently at the door while he clipped the leash on her collar. "All right, girl, let's go make sure that nosy reporter doesn't get herself killed."

It only took him a few minutes to get to the base hospital. He left Annie in her temperature-controlled area of the car and headed inside the building. A stop at the information desk provided him the room number.

Once on the floor, he made a right at the nurses' station and found the room. The door was cracked open and he could hear voices inside.

"Come on, Bobby, please tell me what you know. Do

you know who the guy was?" he heard Heidi ask. "The one who ran from the building?"

"No."

The trainer's low voice vibrated with tension.

Heidi sighed. "That explosion was no coincidence. You know as well as I do about all the weird stuff happening on the base. The Red Rose Killer who killed those two trainers, Clinton Lockwood, and then all of the dogs getting out."

Nick pursed his lips. Those dogs. Out of the twenty-one still missing, he would have thought they would have located a few by now. And those four highly trained German shepherds should have come back. But they hadn't. Which probably meant someone had them.

Uncomfortable with his eavesdropping, he knocked.

"Come in," Bobby called.

Nick stepped inside and found the trainer sitting up in the bed and Heidi in the chair next to him. She raised a brow when she saw him. "What are you doing here?"

"Me? What are you doing here?"

"I thought I'd stop by and check on Bobby." She shot the man in the bed a warm smile and something twisted inside Nick. Something he could only identify as jealousy. But he knew that couldn't possibly be true. His only explanation for the unexpected—and unwelcome—feeling was that he'd had far too little sleep last night. And *every* night since the Red Rose Killer had struck the base and set off a chain of events with the murder of the two trainers as well as of his former Basic Training Commander, Chief Master Sergeant Clinton Lockwood. Since then Boyd Sullivan had continued his reign of terror over those who had any connection with him at all.

Nick cleared his throat. "Do you mind if I join you?"

Heidi shrugged, but Dobby shifted on the bed and wouldn't meet his eyes. Interesting.

"I thought I'd see how he was doing and ask him a few questions about the bombing," Heidi said. "Unfortunately, he doesn't remember much."

"I see. How are you feeling?" Nick asked Bobby.

"I'm all right." The young man seemed grateful for the distraction. "They tell me I should make a full recovery, so that's a relief."

"I'm sure." Nick settled himself in the window seat. "I've got a few questions for you myself, if you don't mind." Without giving the man a chance to answer, he said, "What was your shift at the training center yesterday?"

"Second."

"So, what do you think the man in the building wanted? The one Heidi saw run out?"

Bobby looked away again, over Nick's shoulder and out the window. "I was… I needed a break so I was going to step outside for a breath of fresh air and that's when I saw Heidi. She yelled at me to run." He shrugged and briefly met Nick's eyes. "She sounded really intense, so I ran." He turned his gaze back to Heidi. "You saved my life."

Heidi smiled. Nick ran a hand over his jaw. "So, no idea who the man was?"

"No. I've already said it several times. I've got no idea." The young man plucked at the sheet near his knee. Then he linked his hands and turned his gaze to the television, effectively dismissing them.

Nick frowned. Bobby was lying. He slid a glance over at Heidi and saw her eyes on the man. Her wrinkled forehead said she wasn't buying his story, either.

But why would he lie? Was he somehow involved in

the explosion or did he know the identity of the bomber and was too scared to tell?

A knock on the door brought a flicker of relief to Bobby's pale features. A woman in her midfifties entered. The lab coat and blue lettering stitched on her shoulder identified her as the doctor. "What's going on in here?" she asked.

Nick stood. "We're just having a chat with your patient."

"Well, you're going to have to leave. In case you haven't noticed, he has a head injury and needs his rest."

"We've noticed." He turned to Bobby. "Thank you for your time. If you remember anything else, will you give me a call?" He handed him his card.

"Ah…sure. Yes, of course." He stared at it, then set it on the table by the phone.

"Get better, Bobby. I'm glad you're going to be okay," Heidi said.

Bobby's gaze softened when he turned to look at her and, once again, Nick's blood pressure surged. He shook his head and told himself to get a grip. He was not attracted to her. *Liar.* Okay, fine, so he was, but that was neither here nor there. The only reason he was going to keep an eye on Heidi was to make sure she didn't wind up a victim of the bomber—and to make sure she didn't report anything she shouldn't.

Maybe if he told himself that enough times, he'd eventually believe it.

Once outside the hospital room, Heidi turned to Nick and crossed her arms. "What was that all about?"

"What do you mean?"

"I mean, I was in the middle of a conversation with Bobby and you showed up to interfere."

"You mean you were in the middle of pumping a poor, wounded man for information so you could get a scoop on a story."

"I already got the scoop. I was going for the follow-up," she said.

He blinked. Then laughed and held up a hand in surrender. "I can't believe I'm laughing. I should be really annoyed with you."

"So why aren't you?"

His blue eyes flashed with something she couldn't identify. "I don't really know," he said softly.

"That bothers you, doesn't it?"

"In more ways than I'd like."

She waited for him to explain, but he simply sighed and looked away.

"You don't trust me, do you?" she asked, then raised a hand. "Never mind. Don't answer that. It's as clear as the nose on your face what you think of me."

He gave a short laugh. "You're a reporter. That automatically puts you on the *Do Not Trust* list."

"What happened?"

His brow lifted. "What do you mean?"

"What made you not trust reporters?"

And just like that, his face closed up. "It doesn't matter. It doesn't have anything to do with you or this case, so—"

Her phone buzzed and he snapped his lips shut.

"Sorry," she said. She looked at the screen. "I've got to answer this. It's my boss."

"Of course." The coolness in his voice pierced her, but she swiped the screen and lifted the phone to her ear. "Hello?"

"Heidi, where are you?" Lou Sanders demanded.

"Still at the hospital. I just finished talking to Bobby

Stevens, the man who was hurt in the training center explosion."

"Right. Well, forget about him for now. Three more homes were burglarized last night, medals were stolen and you're needed to conduct interviews and cover the story."

Heidi bit her lip on the complaint that wanted to slip out. Instead, she nodded. "All right. Text me the addresses, and I'll get on it."

"Good. I expect something on my desk by the end of the day tomorrow."

"Yes, sir."

She hung up and found Nick staring at his phone. He tucked it into the clip on his belt. "I've got to get to a meeting. Are you going to be all right?"

"I think so. Nothing's happened, and last night was peaceful."

"I hate leaving you alone."

His concern sent warmth coursing through her. He might not trust her simply because of her profession, but he obviously cared about her as a person. How long had it been since someone had been genuinely concerned about what happened to her? A man, anyway. She had friends on the base, of course, and she and her neighbor, Felicity, had gotten pretty close over the last month in spite of the fact that Westley, her new husband, didn't seem to like Heidi very much. Heidi was glad Felicity was willing to give her the benefit of the doubt.

Heidi waved off his worry. "I'll be fine. I'm going to be working on this story, so I'll be talking with people all day. The base is as busy as a hive. If I need something, someone is within yelling distance at all times."

Nick nodded. "Okay, just be careful."

"Of course."

He didn't move.

She raised a brow. "Now what's wrong?"

"What was your impression of Bobby?" he asked.

"He's in pain and he's lying through his teeth. He knows something, and he's scared to tell what it is. I'm not sure why he's scared, but he is."

"Yeah. That was my take on him, too. What makes you think so, though?"

With a shrug, she said, "He never actually said he didn't see the guy at the center. He never asked me to describe the man I saw. He just denied knowing who the guy was. Which makes me think he did see him and doesn't want to say."

"That's impressive, Heidi."

"Thanks?"

"No, I'm serious. You're perceptive. That's how a cop thinks."

She laughed. "Well, I'm no cop, that's for sure—and I have no desire to be one. Too dangerous."

Her wry statement and roll of her eyes seemed to amuse him.

"Right. Because being a reporter has kept you safe and sound thus far."

"I like my job and I like to do it well. Part of that entails being able to read people and to read in between the lines."

"Which tells me that OSI needs to dig a little deeper into Bobby's background."

"I'd say so."

"I'll give them the rundown on our visit with Airman Stevens." With a nod and one last look in her direction, he turned on his heel and headed down the hallway to the elevator.

Heidi sucked in a breath and told her feelings to

settle down. Yes, Nick was a good-looking man. Yes, she was attracted to him. And no, nothing was going to come of that because…because he didn't respect her occupation, for one. He was bossy and demanding, for two. And he'd awakened long-dormant dreams of what could one day be. A family. A home with children and a husband who loved her—in spite of her job.

With a groan, she knew this was going to be a long day. But at least the interviews would distract her from thinking about the handsome lieutenant. Maybe.

Nick felt slightly better about leaving Heidi. She was right. The base was teeming with people during the day and she'd be with someone constantly on her interviews.

But still…he couldn't shake from his mind the fact that Heidi could be in danger and it was only a matter of time before someone showed up to do her harm.

The guy who'd run from them—and pulled a gun on them—was still out there.

Unable to just drive away, he waited until she came out of the building and watched as she set off on foot. He continued to observe, noting the others leaving at the same time. No one seemed to be following her and that allowed him to draw in a relieved breath and relax a fraction.

Nick then climbed into his vehicle. Annie welcomed him back with a "woof" and he gave her ears a scratch. He drove to the base command office and found a parking spot outside the building that housed the large auditorium-style conference room. Once he was inside, Annie at his side, the executive assistant to the base commander, Brenda Blakenship, met him in the reception area. After they exchanged salutes, she nodded to the nearest door. "Everyone's here. Captain Blackwood is ready."

"Thank you." This was a last-minute meeting on a Saturday. Obviously, something was important.

When he entered the conference room, the large oval table was full of those investigating the Boyd Sullivan case. He saluted and took his seat next to Security Forces Captain Justin Blackwood. Annie settled at his feet with a contented sigh while Nick studied Justin. The captain was a tall, imposing figure, his blond hair cut with military precision. His blue eyes could slice right through a person, but Nick liked the man. In fact, he liked and respected every person in the room. They made a good team. Which was why he knew they would have Boyd Sullivan in custody soon. They had to. This whole investigation had gone on too long.

Across from him sat First Lieutenant Vanessa Gomez, whose insight into Sullivan could be helpful. It was a long shot, but worth having her on the team. Sitting beside her was Captain Gretchen Hill, who had been temporarily transferred to the base to learn how the K-9 Unit and a large security force were run. She'd been assigned to work with Justin, whose former partner had been killed. Nick briefly wondered how that was going. They both looked slightly stressed whenever they were in the same room together. But it wasn't any of his business. They were professionals; they'd work through any problems. Tech Sergeant Linc Colson, a Security Forces investigator, First Lieutenant MP Ethan Webb, Westley James, Ava Esposito and Oliver Davison rounded out the team.

"Thank you all for coming in," base commander Lieutenant General Nathan Hall said. He stood to Nick's left. "I know it's Saturday, but I wanted us all together for an update. It's no secret that Boyd Sullivan is still out there causing grief. He's a killer who shows no mercy and it's up to us to stop him. Fast. First order of business, I think we need to focus a little closer on Yvette Crenville. I still think she's our link. It's well-known how crazy she was about Sullivan, and he seemed to return the feeling."

"True," Nick said. "But we've been looking into her. What else do you suggest?"

"Closer scrutiny. I want constant eyes on her. I want proof supporting our suspicions. I've done some checking and she's regular as clockwork to show up for work, so it should be easy enough to keep her under surveillance. Any volunteers to trail her and report back her routine, who she talks to, where she goes, et cetera?"

Several hands went up and the lieutenant general pointed to Vanessa. "Since you're at the hospital where Yvette works, you're the obvious choice, but are you sure you're up to it?"

"Yes, sir. I'll have to work around my schedule, of course, but I'm happy to do it when I'm not on the clock. Then again, she *is* the base nutritionist, so I may be able to catch up to her occasionally during the day, to see if she's up to anything suspicious."

"All right, you're on it. The only reason I'm asking is because when Ava and Oliver were searching for Turner Johnson last month, they spotted Sullivan in the woods." Seven-year-old Turner Johnson, the son of a base colonel, had been on a school field trip when he'd disappeared. Ava Esposito and Oliver Davison had brought the child home safely. "Turner talked about the 'bad guy and mean woman.' Unfortunately, he never got a look at her. She had on a black hoodie and stuff. But he was sure it was a woman. So, by process of elimination, we're down to Yvette. If it's her, she's going to be suspicious of anyone in law enforcement. But she wouldn't have any reason to connect you to the investigation," he told Vanessa.

"No, we've talked a couple of times, and she knows I got a rose as well." Yvette had received one the same night as Vanessa.

"But I don't want you doing this alone. I think you're safe at the hospital, surrounded by people, but I'm going to find someone to partner with you. When I decide who it'll be, I'll let you know."

"That sounds good, sir. I do feel safe at the hospital." Vanessa shrugged. "It might be a false sense of security, but for now, I think I'm all right."

"Good, let me know if anything changes."

"Of course."

For the next thirty minutes, the team discussed the case in detail. With one glaring, depressing fact right in front of them. Boyd Sullivan was still on the loose and no one had any idea where he was or how to find him.

"One last thing," Lieutenant General Hall said. "Our anonymous blogger is still wreaking havoc. This time he—or she—has decided to smear the investigators all over the place."

"What do you mean, sir?" Nick asked.

Nathan tapped his phone's screen and read from the blog, "'Well, folks, it looks like the training center bombing wasn't just a random thing. There's speculation that the Red Rose Killer is somehow involved. That it's possible he's back on base. Lock your doors, folks. I know I'm going to.'" Nathan tossed his phone on the table. "I want this person stopped."

"Whoever it is has mad tech skills," Nick said. "But there's got to be more to it."

"What do you mean?"

"I'm just saying, it's like this person has a bug planted in our meetings. We've talked about everything the blogger's mentioned. As we've noted, these are confidential discussions that are being plastered in the posts. I think it's time to play our cards a little closer to our vests." He looked around. "I'm not saying it's one of us, but I do think it's someone we're trusting."

Justin scowled. "Then from this moment on, trust no one but the people in this room. Discuss nothing, and I mean nothing, about this case with anyone but the people here. Is that understood?"

A chorus of "Yes, sirs" echoed through the small room. "Good. That's it for now. Stay in touch."

Most everyone filed out, but Nathan reached out to Nick. "Hang back, will you? You, too, Justin, Gretchen."

With a raised brow, Nick glanced at Gretchen, who shrugged and shoved a strand of short dark hair behind her ear and then tucked it up under the blue beret.

After the others were gone, Nathan turned to them. "Gretchen, what do you think about pairing up with Vanessa in order to keep eyes on Yvette at all times?"

"I'm happy to do it," she said.

"I know that we had considered Vanessa might actually be Boyd's accomplice. I truly don't think she is, but I'd feel better knowing you were observing. And not only that, it's possible she's a target since she got a rose and a note. I'd like someone watching her back as well."

"Absolutely. I agree."

"What do you think, Nick?"

"I think that's a great idea. We don't need to take any unnecessary chances with anyone's life."

"Good, that's settled, then. Gretchen, why don't you catch up with Vanessa and let her in on the plan?"

"Of course, sir." She hurried off.

Once she was gone, Nick raked a hand over his crew cut. "I think we need eyes on Heidi Jenks as well."

"You think she's up to something?"

"No. I think she's in danger." He didn't bother explaining why he thought that. Nathan and Justin were both aware of everything that had happened last night.

Nathan pursed his lips, then nodded. "All right. Why don't you take on that responsibility?"

"Yes, sir. Happy to."

"Excellent. I still want you to be a part of the investigative team, but my gut's telling me Heidi needs to be a priority. Until we know for sure she's safe, you and Annie stay close to her."

"Yes, sir." He paused. "One more thing. I know OSI is investigating the bombing of the training center and is keeping you in the loop."

"Right."

"Heidi and I saw the trainer who was hurt in the blast, Bobby Stevens."

"How's he doing?"

"Recovering. But he's lying about something."

Justin raised a brow. "How's that?"

Nick told them about the visit. "I think he and Heidi have established some sort of bond, simply because she's the one who warned him to run in time and saved his life. But he's hiding something even from her."

"Hiding what? The identity of the person who set the explosion?"

"Maybe. He claims he doesn't know who it was. I think he does know, but is too scared to say anything.

Maybe." He shook his head. "I don't know what it is, but there's something."

"You want to do some digging?" Justin asked.

"I can. I don't want to step on OSI's toes, though."

"I think as long as you agree to share whatever you find out, they'll be all right," the Lieutenant said.

"Of course."

Justin nodded. "See if Heidi will agree to continue to keep that bond with Stevens. Maybe at some point he'll tell her what he's hiding."

"That wasn't really what I was thinking, but I can do that."

"What were you thinking?"

"That someone needs to do an in-depth background check on him."

"They did that when he enlisted," Nathan said.

"I know, sir, but I still think he needs to be investigated. Finances, daily routine, the people he hangs out with and socializes with."

"So, a full-blown investigation," Justin said, rubbing his chin.

"Exactly, sir."

"I'll mention your concerns to Agent Steffen."

"Thank you."

Nick left, satisfied that everyone seemed to be in agreement that Heidi needed protection—and that he was the guy for the job. He told himself that his happiness had nothing to do with the fact that he wanted to see Heidi again and everything to do with the fact that he just wanted to make sure she stayed safe. He'd feel the same about anyone in her situation.

Liar.

He huffed a sigh and decided not to examine any of that too closely.

He'd keep Heidi safe and that would be that.

So, why was he wondering what her favorite flower was?

Nick put the mental brakes on once again.

No flowers, no romance, no nothing. Why did he have to keep reminding himself of that when it came to her? He hadn't had that problem until she kept crossing his path. Now, when he thought about the future, blue eyes and shoulder-length wavy blond hair kept intruding. It was ridiculous. She was a reporter. The one profession that filled him with disgust.

No flowers, no romance, no nothing.

But takeout wasn't included in that list. He'd grab some Chinese and stop by to check on her. Just to be sure she was safe. Chinese wasn't romantic.

Unless he included candles.

"No candles, Donovan," he muttered. "Get your mind off romance and on keeping her safe."

After all, he had a direct order to that effect.

FOUR

"Thank you for seeing me, Mrs. Weingard." Heidi stood on the front porch of the house and smiled at the woman who'd answered her knock.

Children's voices echoed loudly behind her. The young mother nodded and swiped a stray hair from her eyes and turned. "Billy! Stop jumping on the couch and take your sisters upstairs."

"Can we play video games?"

"Yes, for a little while."

Screams of glee at the apparently unexpected treat trailed behind the youngsters as they raced up the steps. A door slammed. Silence descended. "Call me Kitty," the woman said. "And come in if you dare."

Heidi stepped into the chaos. And longing pierced her. Would she ever have a family to call her own? With children who would leave their toys strewn around the furniture and the floor in testament to a play-filled afternoon?

Heidi wasn't getting any younger, and she had to admit that as the months passed, the questions seemed to rear their heads more and more. First Lieutenant Nick Donovan's flashing blue eyes popped into her mind for a split second and she cleared her throat. "You look like you stay busy."

Kitty laughed. "Are you kidding me? I rarely get to sit down, that's for sure." She paused. "But I love them. They're high-energy, but have sweet dispositions. Do you have kids?"

"No, not yet. Hopefully, one day."

Kitty picked up a children's book, two toy trucks and a plastic tiara from the couch. Then waved a hand at it. "Have a seat."

Perched on the edge of the cushion, Heidi pulled her voice-activated recorder from her bag. "Do you mind if I record this? It makes it easier to just transcribe everything later." It also was proof if someone discounted her reporting.

"Sure, that's fine."

"So, can you start from the beginning?"

"Um...like I told the police, my husband was deployed a few weeks ago for his third tour to Afghanistan. He's earned a purple heart and other medals that we kept in a drawer in the bedroom. I'd gone grocery shopping while my kids were at school and when I got home, I found the house torn apart."

"So, this happened during broad daylight."

"Exactly."

"And no one noticed anything at all?"

She shrugged. "No, I think the MPs questioned the neighbors and looked at the security camera footage, but all they could see was a guy in a black hoodie strolling casually out my front door, with his hands tucked in his pockets."

"A black hoodie, huh?"

"Yes."

Like the guy who'd bombed the training center? Sounded like him.

Heidi continued to question the woman, but her mind was only halfway on the interview as she really wanted to know if the training center bomber, the guy who'd pulled the gun at her home, and the person stealing the medals were one and the same. Although it didn't make much sense to her. Why go from stealing medals to bombing an unused portion of the training center? What could be the purpose in that?

Soon, she wrapped up and tucked her recorder back into her purse.

Kitty stood. "Do you think my story will help?"

"I don't know. But it sure won't hurt. The more people who are aware of what is going on, the more likely they are to keep their eyes open."

"I suppose. You know, the thefts are sad and it's infuriating that someone would do such a thing. I'm more angry about the disrespect to my husband and the other soldiers than the loss of the medals. They aren't worth much. Maybe a couple hundred dollars each. But what they represent…that's priceless. And stealing them just makes me mad."

"I agree completely," Heidi said. "Unfortunately, a few of the medals that have been stolen have been passed down through the generations and are worth quite a bit of money. I think the thief is just taking his chances with the value. He doesn't know who has what, but finds something worthwhile to keep stealing more. And, also, a few hundred dollars times a hundred-plus medals is some nice pocket change. In addition to the jewelry and money he finds on top of the medals."

"True. But it sure makes my blood boil."

"I understand. Hopefully, this person will be in custody soon and everyone can relax." On that score, any-way. With Sullivan still on the loose, no one would be relaxing anytime soon. Heidi walked to the door. "Thanks again for meeting with me. If you think of anything else, please give me a call." She held out her card.

"Of course."

"Mom! Can we have some popcorn?"

"In just a minute, hon," Kitty called over her shoulder to her son.

"Thanks! And some apple juice boxes?"

"Yes, I'll bring them in a minute if you won't interrupt again, please."

"Okay."

The door slammed again and Kitty rolled her eyes, but the smile curving her lips said she didn't really mind. She looked tired as most moms with multiple children were, but it was obvious she loved her brood. The longing hit Heidi again, and she had to push it away, yet again. It would happen for her. Someday. Maybe.

Heidi left and headed for the next interview, where she heard basically the same story as Mrs. Weingard's, except the break-in had occurred at night when the newly married couple had gone to dinner. The thief had taken the young man's great-grandfather's Medal of Valor, awarded to him by the President of the United States for his service in World War II. The young groom almost cried as he described the loss, and Heidi's heart ached for him.

Hours later, she decided to call it a day. It had been a long one and she was exhausted from the emotional roller coaster she'd ridden while doing the interviews. She'd done her best to offer comfort and sympathy, and now she needed some space to gather her notes and write the article.

Walking home, Heidi felt slightly guilty once again. While listening to Airman Keith Bull talk about his great-grandfather with pride gleaming in his gray eyes, it had occurred to her that she was doing the story—and the families—a disservice with her lack of focus. They deserved her full attention even if the stolen medals story hadn't been her first choice for an assignment.

So she didn't get the lead on the Red Rose Killer story.

So her boss couldn't seem to see past his own nose—or his obvious favorite, John Robinson—to see her potential.

So John Robinson drove her batty.

So what?

She was a good reporter and she needed to give this story her best. The families deserved that.

Decision made, guilt assuaged, she drew in a deep breath of the night air. As the sun dipped lower on the horizon, the temperature dropped. She loved being outside in the fall. It was time to open the windows and turn the air-conditioning off. And write.

She strode with a little more pep in her step, actually looking forward to transcribing her notes and sending this article to Lou.

Footsteps sounded behind her and she spun. The setting sun blinded her for a moment, but she thought she saw a shadow dart off to the right and slip down the sidewalk that led to more houses off the main Base Boulevard.

Chills swept through her. That was weird. And creepy. And secretive. For a moment, she considered searching for the shadow, but memories of icy blue eyes, exploding buildings and the man with the gun steered her steps toward home. Quick steps. Sure, she could

Just be paranoid, but that didn't mean someone wasn't following her. One blessing was that there were plenty of people out tonight enjoying the weather. She passed several officers and saluted, thankful for their presence on the sidewalk.

But the darting shadow still bothered her.

A hand on her shoulder spun her around and she let out a startled squeal. She raised a fist and swung it— only to have it caught.

"Heidi! It's just me, Nick."

He released her hand and she placed it over her racing heart. "Wow. You scared me. Seriously?"

"I called your name twice. You started walking faster."

"I didn't hear you. But a few minutes ago, I thought someone was following me." She frowned. "When I turned, he shot off down a side street."

"I must have crossed the street about then because I saw you turn around. Where are you headed?"

"Home."

"Do you mind if I walk with you?"

Was he kidding? "That would be great, thanks." She looked behind him. "Where's Annie?"

"Back at the kennel. She's finished her work for the day so she gets to take a break."

Once they were inside her home, she kicked off her shoes and turned on a lamp. And sniffed. The trash in the kitchen. Great. It wasn't horrible, but it wasn't great. She'd meant to take it out first thing that morning, but in all of the chaos of everything, she'd forgotten. Oh, well. Hopefully, he wouldn't judge her. "Want something to drink?" she asked him.

"Sure. Whatever you've got is fine."

She returned with two glasses of iced tea. He took

his and settled on the couch. She turned her air conditioner off and opened the two windows in the den to let in the fresh air, then took the recliner. "Any progress on finding the man who blew up the center?" she asked.

"No. Unfortunately. And nothing on Sullivan, either. That man is as slippery as a snake."

"As scary as one, too." She shuddered.

"Depends on the snake," he said. "How's the story coming with the stolen medals?"

She shrugged. "I'm talking to the victims. The MPs are tight-lipped about the investigation so I have to get the details from the people who'll talk to me."

"People don't trust reporters. Especially law enforcement."

"No kidding. At least not until it suits their purposes, then they're the first ones to call."

He tilted his head. "How do you live with that? Doesn't it get frustrating?"

"Of course."

"So, why do it? Why pick a career that a lot of people don't have a lot of respect for?"

She sighed. "Because it's in my blood. My father was a reporter and a good one. He was killed while investigating a story and after the shock wore off, the anger set in. I was mad. Livid. It felt like if I could pick up where he left off, I would be carrying on his legacy." She shrugged "I don't know if that makes any sense or not."

"Strangely enough, it kind of does."

His soft words pierced the chunk of armor she'd had to wrap around her heart. "Thank you."

He cleared his throat and nodded.

"And besides," she said, "journalism is a very respectful career. It's just a few who give it a bad name. I'm trying to be one of the good ones."

"I'm starting to see that," he said softly.

"You are?"

"Yeah."

"Well, good. Thanks." They fell silent and she studied him for a moment.

"What is it? You're looking at me weirdly."

"I was wondering what happened to you."

"What do you mean?"

"You're very anti-media, anti-reporters. More so than what seems normal for the average person, I guess. I figure something must have happened to make you feel that way."

Nick looked away. She'd brought the subject up before and he'd managed to avoid answering. He didn't like to talk about his mother's death to anyone. Much less a reporter. Then again, she could easily research it and find out everything she wanted to know and more. Of course, most of it wouldn't be truth. And he wanted her to know the truth.

For a moment, he wondered why he cared. When he couldn't come up with an acceptable answer, he shook his head. "My mother was a Type 1 diabetic. She'd battled the disease from the age of eight. But she did well, got married and had me. My father was a political star and rising through the ranks in Washington when a reporter took pictures of him in a very compromising position with his young and very pretty political assistant."

Heidi's eyes widened. "Uh-oh."

"Exactly. Those pictures wound up in the newspapers and all the media outlets you can think of and his career was destroyed."

"I'm sorry."

His eyes frosted. "Are you? Are you saying you

wouldn't have done the same thing had you been in that reporter's place?"

She bit her lip. "I'm sorry it happened. Would I have done the same thing?" She frowned. "I don't know."

"Right."

With narrowed eyes, she did her best to filter her response. "Look, until I'm walking in someone else's shoes, I can't tell you what I would or wouldn't do in that same situation. I *can* tell you that I do my best to act with integrity at all times. I get that not all reporters have the same code of honor, but I do." She paused. "Was the story fact or not?"

"Fact."

She huffed. "Then, yes. I might have done the same thing."

He stood and shoved his hands in his pockets as he checked the locks on her windows.

"Where's your father now?" she asked him.

"Married to that assistant and living in San Antonio. She's sixteen years younger than he is."

"Do you talk to him?"

"No. Not often. He doesn't seem to care."

She winced. "Nick, I'm sorry you had a rough time, I really am. It's no fun being in the spotlight, I get that. Trust me. Probably better than you think."

He turned to her. "You're talking about when your dad was killed?"

"Yes."

"Where's your mother?"

"Happily remarried to a pastor, living in Tennessee."

"Nice."

"It is." She sighed. "But if the story about your father was fact, why are you so antagonistic?"

"Because it led to my mother's death. Indirectly."

She blinked. "Oh. How?"

"The story led to her depression, which led to her not taking care of herself, which led to her insulin issues going out of control, which led to her passing out at the wheel and going over a cliff.

"Anyway, that was one story the papers got all wrong because a diabetic passing out at the wheel and driving over a cliff isn't nearly as sensational as saying she killed herself. And that's the conclusion they immediately came to when there were no skid marks indicating she tried to stop."

With a gasp, Heidi surged to her feet. "That's horrible, Nick."

She sounded like she meant it.

"Horrible is one way to describe it," he said.

"And completely unethical. I'm so sorry. I really am."

He raked a hand over his hair. "I am, too." And why was he telling her this?

"Did you confront the reporter?" she asked.

"I did, actually. He didn't care and there was nothing I could do to make him grow a conscience. There was no way to prove Mom didn't commit suicide—even though the autopsy later revealed that her blood sugar was so low that she probably passed out. But even with that evidence in hand, the paper wouldn't print a retraction or admit they might have jumped the gun and not done a thorough investigation before printing the story. But Mom wasn't suicidal. She was hurt and she was mad at my dad and aggravated with the media up to that point, but she'd just bought us tickets to go see the Rangers play at the stadium that weekend." He gave her a short smile. "We were big fans." He sighed. Enough. He didn't come over here to go down memory lane.

He turned away and once again examined her windows. Maybe just to give himself something to do. "Do you have an alarm system?" he asked.

"Um, no. Why?"

"Because I think you probably need one."

With a slow nod, she let her gaze sweep around her home. "I've never felt unsafe here. This place has been my sanctuary since I moved in. And now…" She rubbed her arms. "I feel like a sitting duck."

"We'll work on that. What are your plans tomorrow?"

She shrugged. "Church, then lunch. Sometimes Felicity and I see a movie if Westley is busy. Other times I ride out to the lake. I'll probably work some in the afternoon after I make my weekly call to Mom and take a nap. And then I have that last interview I need to do with the latest theft victim so I can get this article in to Lou."

"You don't have many friends, I gather," he said softly.

She gave him a sad smile. "Well, I had a few more, but when rumors of me being the anonymous blogger started gaining some traction, a lot of them kind of dropped off the radar."

His jaw tightened. He didn't want to feel sympathy for her. And yet, he did. "We go to the same church here on base. So…come to church with me tomorrow and let's grab lunch after."

Her eyes went wide, then narrowed. "Wait a minute. Is this pity company?"

He blinked. "What?"

"You know. You feel sorry for me, so you're trying to do something nice. Not because you really want to, but because you feel you should."

His jaw dropped and for a moment, he just stared at her. Then he stood and glared, jabbing a finger at her.

"I don't do pity company. Sure, I feel bad that you're feeling the brunt of the gossip, but I don't spend time with people because I feel sorry for them." Much. Okay, maybe occasionally, but that didn't apply to this situation. "And if I do," he said, completely negating what he'd just claimed, "I don't volunteer to spend *that* much time with them." Her eyes sparkled, and he cleared his throat—something he found himself doing a lot around her. "Anyway, no. Definitely not pity company."

His glower didn't seem to faze her. She searched his eyes. "I think I believe you," she said. Then grinned.

Having her throw his words back at him sent his anger down the drain. A bark of laughter escaped him and he stepped back. "Well, thank you, ma'am. I appreciate that."

A small smile tugged at her lips. "You're welcome."

"So? Church and lunch?"

"Sure," she said. "Church and lunch."

"Good. I'll pick you up." With that, he left her standing in her den, staring after him, speechless.

The smile on his face died when he saw the Security Forces vehicle parked outside her home. Nope, not pity company. Protective company, yes. Because while he had no plans to fall for the pretty reporter, he was genuinely worried about her safety. He sighed and did a one-eighty. Back at her door, he knocked.

She opened it with a frown. "Are you okay?"

"Yes. I just need to know your favorite flower."

"Pink carnations. Why?"

"Just needed to know. See you tomorrow."

"But—"

"Good night, Heidi."

Her confused huff made him smile again. A tight smile that stayed with him all the way home.

When he stepped inside, he found his grandfather in the recliner, a football game playing on the television mounted over the fireplace. A retired colonel, the man had moved in with him after Nick's grandmother had died last year. He was able to function on his own, but Nick felt better with him there so he could keep an eye on him. And besides, he liked the company. "Hey, Gramps, how's it going?"

"It's going fine. Where've you been?"

"I went over to see Heidi." He'd told his grandfather about the explosion. As much as he could, anyway. Even though the man was retired military, there were still things Nick had to keep to himself. "I was worried about her."

"Uh-huh. You like her, don't you?"

"Did you miss the part where I said she's a reporter?"

"I didn't miss it. So why do you like her?"

"I didn't say I did."

Gramps harrumphed and let out a low laugh. "Okay, boy."

His grandfather could make him feel like a child of ten without even trying. "Gramps…"

"I picked up your shirts from the cleaners. You can wear the blue one tomorrow to church."

Church. Right. "Ah…about church. We have to swing by and pick up Heidi. She's going with us."

"That reporter you don't like?"

He sighed. "Yes, sir, that's the one."

"Gotta find me a woman I don't like as much as you don't like that one."

With a groan, Nick made his way back to his room and shut the door on his grandfather's chuckles.

"Just keeping her safe, that's it," he muttered to the quiet room. Because in spite of the lighthearted banter with his grandfather, Nick's pulse pounded a rhythm of fear every time he thought about her being a target of the man who bombed the training center.

Which meant nothing special, he told himself. He'd be concerned about anyone who'd caught the attention of a man who bombed a building.

But Heidi...

He did like Heidi. A lot.

And while his head argued that it was a bad idea, his heart was jumping all over it.

He had a feeling he was in big trouble.

FIVE

Heidi had found sleep difficult to come by last night, but when nothing had happened by one o'clock, and she could see the MP was still parked outside, she'd been able to fall into a restless doze. By the time her alarm buzzed, she was already up and getting ready.

And questioning her sanity as she slicked pink gloss across her lips. "We go to the same church here on base. So…come to church with me tomorrow and let's grab lunch after."

She rolled her eyes at her reflection and decided she would do. She'd left her hair down and it rested against her shoulders, the strands straightened with the help of her flat iron. Light makeup enhanced her blue eyes and the lip gloss added a subtle sheen to her mouth.

In her day-to-day work life, she looked professional and neat, not made-up. It suited her. So why was she making more of an effort today?

She knew exactly why and his name was Nick Donovan. She might as well admit it.

With a grimace, she turned from the sink and headed for the kitchen for a bagel and a cup of coffee. Her nose reminded her she still needed to take the trash out, but she wasn't about to risk dirtying her nice clothes. She put that at the top of her after-church to-do list. A glance out the window revealed the Security Forces vehicle still parked on her street. She frowned. The man she'd seen running from the training center hadn't liked that she'd seen his face. In fact, he'd been so desperate to get away he'd pulled a gun on her and Nick. Then he'd managed to escape the base perimeter. Would he come back or was his work done? Or had he decided the smart thing to do was disappear? She hoped it was the latter.

While she was on her second cup, her phone rang, and she snagged it. "Hi, Mom."

"Hey, stranger."

Heidi grimaced. "Sorry, it's been crazy around here."

"I know. I've been keeping up with what's happening on the base. They haven't caught that serial killer yet. Boyd Sullivan."

"No, they haven't, but they don't think he's on the base anymore. He was last seen in central Texas."

"And what about the explosion at the training center?" her mother asked.

"Oh. You heard about that, huh?"

"Like I said, I keep up."

What could she say that would be the truth, but not send her mother running to the base?

"We're not sure, Mom. OSI is investigating so we hope we hear something soon. Until then, security is super tight."

"I would hope so. Do you need to take a leave of absence and come here?"

"No, ma'am. I need to stay here and do my job."

"In spite of the fact that it might get you killed?"

"I'm not planning on putting myself in any danger."

"Your father—"

"Dad knew exactly what he was walking into when

he started working that story. Now that I'm older, I understand his thought processes. He didn't want to die, but he was doing what he believed in." She paused. "I'm not Dad, but I'm a lot like him. I don't plan to do anything that may put me in danger, but I believe in ferreting out the truth."

For a moment her mother didn't respond and Heidi wondered if she would hang up on her. Then a watery sigh reached her. "On the contrary, my dear, you are just like your father."

"Well...okay."

"And I'm very proud of you."

Heidi snapped her mouth shut. Then let out a low sigh. "Thanks, Mom. I needed to hear that."

"Please let me know if there's anything I can do."

"I will."

"And someone needs to tell that blogger to quit posting. Whoever is writing that stuff is revealing things probably better kept under wraps."

A choked laugh escaped her. "I agree, Mom. They're working on silencing that person."

"Which means they don't know who it is."

"You're very astute."

Heidi could almost hear the smile her mother no doubt wore. "I love you, hon."

A knock on the door made her jump. "I love you, too, Mom. We'll talk later, okay? Give Kurt my best." She really did like her stepfather. Mostly because he adored her mother.

"Of course."

"Bye." Heidi hung up as another knock echoed through her small home. She rose and placed the cup in the sink, then grabbed her purse.

When she opened the door, she blinked. Nick in his

military fatigues was one thing, but dressed in civilian clothing, he plain looked *good*. Amazing. She'd seen him at church before in his civvies, of course, but to have him standing on her doorstep put a whole different kind of beat in her heart.

"Hi," she said. "Good morning."

"Morning." He blinked as his gaze swept over her. "Wow. You look different."

"Thanks?"

He shook his head and laughed. "Sorry. I mean different as in good."

Did a little makeup make that much of a difference? Apparently, it did, judging by how his eyes were focused on her. "Thank you. You look different, too. As in good."

She thought his cheeks might have gone a little pink. He cleared his throat. "I think I need to work on my manners. Let's start over." He turned his back to her, walked down the steps, then back up. When he stood in front of her once more, he offered her a slight bow. "Heidi, you look lovely this morning."

And there went her heart. "Thank you." She was sure her cheek color now matched his. And where did that breathlessness come from? She cleared her throat. "Is it okay if I don't say 'you do, too'?"

He laughed. "I'm more than fine with not being called lovely. Are you ready?"

"I am." She locked the door, then shut it behind her. Then she smiled up at him. "But you are handsome."

"Ah, thank you." More throat clearing. "I hope you don't mind that we have some company."

"Not at all. Who? Annie?"

"And my grandfather. Colonel Truman Hicks, retired. He lives with me and decided to come to church this morning."

"Sounds wonderful." She hoped it would be, anyway. "So, how does he feel about reporters after what happened to your mother? His daughter, I presume?"

His eyes narrowed. "Yes, he's my mother's father. Let's just say he's reserving judgment on any reporters, present company included."

"Uh-huh."

At the car, he introduced her to the man who sat in the back seat. He looked familiar, like she'd seen him in the church before, but she wouldn't have placed him if Nick hadn't introduced them. "Very nice to meet you, sir, but I'm happy to take the back."

"I've got better manners than that, young lady. Climb in."

"Yes, sir." She raised a brow at Nick and he shrugged and opened the door for her. Oh, boy, this might just get interesting.

Annie rode in the very back. The colonel stayed quiet the entire ride while Nick did an excellent job with small talk. She figured the colonel was listening and observing, because while he didn't seem to resent her presence, she wasn't sure he approved of it.

So, Heidi focused on Nick and thought she managed to sound halfway intelligent. The sight of a handler walking his dog brought the missing animals to mind. "Any word on the dogs still missing from the kennel?" she asked.

"No."

"What about the four German shepherds? Felicity said Westley was especially concerned about them."

"They're definitely the more trained and special

dogs, for sure, but there's been no word or sightings on them. It's frustrating."

"I'm sure."

They fell silent and she couldn't hold back the sigh of relief when the church came into view.

The jaunt from her home to the church had taken all of three minutes. It had felt like at least thirty.

Nick parked and everyone climbed out into the heat that was already starting to steal the oxygen from the air. She was definitely ready for cooler weather.

The colonel went on ahead, his steps confident and sure, his back straight and strong.

"Why'd he retire?" Heidi asked as Nick released Annie from her area. "He seems a little on the young side."

"He is. He'll only be sixty-eight on his next birthday, but a couple of years ago, my grandmother got sick," he said, "and he wanted to give her his full attention so he requested a leave and was granted it. She passed away. Losing my mom and then grandmother was hard for him. Grief knocked him for a loop. He had his forty-five years—and then some—in, so he was able to retire. Since it was just the two of us left in the family, I decided to ask him to move in with me. He didn't argue about it too much. I think he was lonely."

"I see." She walked with him up the steps and into the sanctuary. "You've had a lot of pain in your life."

"Hmm No more than anyone else, probably. Life comes with a guarantee of pain. It's how you deal with it that matters."

"Maybe." He was right, of course. She just didn't want to think about how she'd dealt with the pain life had served her. Avoiding it wasn't exactly dealing with it.

They found their seats. The colonel sat in the front

row. Now she knew why he'd looked familiar. She saw the back of him most Sundays. Nick led her to a pew in the middle and slid in. She sat next to him, ignoring the suddenly speculative looks of some of the others around them. "You don't sit with your grandfather?"

"No. Sometimes I have to slip out and I prefer not to do that in front of the whole congregation. He's sat in that seat since he's been on base so he's not about to move. And see that empty space next to him?"

"Yes."

"He puts Gramma's Bible there in her place."

"He likes tradition."

"Thrives on it."

"And no one says anything? What if a new person sits there without knowing the history?"

He smiled. "Then Gramps finds another place to sit. But the nice thing is, most newcomers don't sit in the front row so it's not an issue."

"Cool." Nick came from a long line of love and an impressive family—at least on his mother's side.

Westley and Felicity slid in beside Nick, then looked around Nick to greet her. "How are you doing? Recovering from the blast, I hope?" Westley asked her.

"I still have sore knees, but other than that, I'm doing fine, thanks."

He nodded and started to say something else, then snapped his lips shut as John Robinson approached. Heidi's stomach turned sour, but she kept her face blank, not wanting the reporter to see her reaction.

"Good morning, all," John said. "Thought I'd catch you here. Master Sergeant James, can you give us an update on the Red Rose Killer?"

"I cannot. Have a nice day, Robinson."

The reporter flinched and narrowed his eyes at Heidi.

"Lou isn't going to be happy to hear about this. This is my story."

Heidi crossed her arms and raised her chin. "Did I say it wasn't?"

"No, but everywhere I go, you're there." His gaze flicked to Nick. "With someone working the investigation. If you're hoping to scoop me on this—" The music started and he was forced to end his bickering. "We'll talk later."

"Not if I can help it," she muttered as John walked across the aisle and Nick placed a comforting hand at the small of her back. She shot him a tight smile and drew in a deep breath that was supposed to help lower her blood pressure.

It helped. A little.

Security Forces Captain Justin Blackwood and his sixteen-year-old daughter, Portia, entered and quickly found a seat. Portia carried her ever-present iPad and looked about as happy to be in church as she would being stuck in after-school detention. Not for the first time, Heidi wondered what her story was or what went through her head—the daughter of a high-ranking military official. But also the daughter of a single dad. From what Heidi had learned just from keeping her ears open around the base, Portia was the result of a high school romance. She'd lived with her mother until the woman had died about a year ago and then Justin had gotten custody. She'd been living with her father ever since and didn't seem at all happy about that fact.

Heidi couldn't remember seeing a smile on the girl's face and that made her sad.

She let her mind flip from the girl to what she needed to do on the Red Rose Killer. While she'd been honest about not working the story, it didn't mean she just had to ignore it, right? Of course, she had her priorities straight. First and foremost, she needed to figure out what was going on with the missing medals, but if she happened to come across something that could lead them to Boyd Sullivan, then so be it. John would stroke out if that happened, but there wasn't anything she could do about that. That was his problem.

When the second song ended and it was time to sit, she realized she hadn't even been aware of standing. However, she was very aware of Nick's hand still at the small of her back. Which made her wish they'd sing at least one more song.

But it wasn't to be.

She sat and continued her musing even as she tried to focus on the sermon and not on the man next to her. And then it hit home what Pastor Harmon was talking about. Something about loving one's enemies. She slid a glance at John Robinson across the aisle and clamped her lips together. *Lord, don't ask me to love him, please. That's going above and beyond, isn't it?* Then her gaze moved to the man on her right. *But Nick Donovan might be another thing altogether.* However, Nick wasn't her enemy, so she was pretty sure that wouldn't be the correct application of the sermon. Still…

"Are you all right?" Nick whispered.

She started. "Yes, why?"

"You're squirmy and distracted. Like a little kid."

Heat suffused her cheeks. "Sorry." For the rest of the service, she sat still as a rock and forced her mind to stay on the sermon.

Once the service ended, they made their way to the back of the church and stood in line to greet the pastor and exit. Annie stayed obediently beside Nick. "She's really an amazing dog, isn't she?" Heidi said.

Nick leaned down to scratch the hound's ears. "Truly amazing. Not very pretty and the slobber sometimes gets to me, but she's all heart and give. I couldn't ask for a better partner."

"I hate that the other dogs are still missing. I hope someone's taking care of them."

He frowned. "I do, too."

"It's been five months since Sullivan released them. Do you think there's still hope?"

"Of course there's hope, Heidi." But it wasn't Nick who answered. It was Pastor Harmon who'd no doubt heard her remark as they approached him. He reached for her hand and gave it a friendly squeeze. "There's always hope—even when the situation looks hopeless."

Heidi smiled at the friendly and wise man she'd come to enjoy speaking with on Sunday afternoons. "Hello, Pastor Harmon. I know God can use even this situation. Sometimes it's hard to focus on that, though."

"I know. I'm praying those dogs come home soon."

"Thank you," Nick said. "We appreciate that." They moved on and stepped out into the heat. "Lunch?" he asked.

"That sounds fabulous."

They found his grandfather talking to three officers and making a golf date. When Heidi and Nick approached, his brown eyes turned speculative. "I'm going to skip out on lunch with you two if that's all right. These three need a fourth."

"Of course, Gramps, just call me if you need a ride home."

"One of these guys can drop me off. Y'all mind?"

"No, sir, happy to do it," one of the officers said. Heidi tried to pull his name from the recesses of her memory, but couldn't find it.

Then Nick's hand was under her elbow and he was leading her to his car. "Is the Winged Java okay with you?"

"Sure. I love their potato soup and Caesar salad."

"Perfect."

They were stopped by Pastor Harmon, who called out Nick's name. He stood at the top of the steps, waving him over.

"Go on, I'll meet you at the car," she said.

The parking lot was almost empty. The car was twenty yards away.

He nodded and jogged over to the steps while she headed for the vehicle. The sound of an engine caught her attention and she turned to see a vehicle heading toward her. Black-tinted windows blocked her view of the driver. As he rode toward her, his window rolled down, his right arm lifted...

...and she saw the semiautomatic in his grasp aimed right at her.

Nick turned at the sound of the first crack from the gun, followed by a *rat-a-tat-tat* that spit up the asphalt near his SUV. "Heidi!" He ran toward her, pulling his weapon. She'd darted behind the vehicle as the weapon fired, but had she been fast enough? "Heidi! Are you hit?"

The silver sedan roared to the edge of the parking lot, then out into the street without stopping. Within seconds, it had sped around the corner.

He turned to see his grandfather on the phone, yelling orders. The MPs would be here soon, but there was no one here to follow the guy. No matter, someone would catch him soon enough. He was on a closed base and wouldn't get far. Nick rounded the side of the vehicle to find Heidi crouching behind a tire. When she saw him, she launched herself into his arms. He held her, his heart thudding with the knowledge that she didn't appear to be harmed.

He pushed her back to look her over. No blood in sight.

"He didn't hit me," she said. "Came close, but I think trying to shoot me from a moving car threw off his aim."

The colonel hurried over, phone still pressed to his ear. "Do we need an ambulance?"

"No, sir," Heidi said, although Nick knew they'd send one anyway. "Let me sit for a minute, please," she said. "My knees are shaking."

He lowered her to the asphalt and knelt beside her. "You're sure you're okay?"

"Just shaken."

"Understandable."

Sirens were already screaming closer, racing down Canyon Drive. Nick tucked his weapon back into his holster as the first Security Forces vehicles turned into the church parking lot. "You'll need to give a statement," he told her.

"I know. I'm just trying to get it together. It's a story, right? I can do this. I can write this from my perspective."

Already she sounded stronger, but Nick was floored. "A story? You were almost killed!"

Her eyes met his as she stood. "I'm aware of that, thanks."

"Apparently not. It's not a story. It's your life!"

"Stop shouting, Nick, and let me handle this my way."

Belatedly, he realized what she was doing. Compartmentalizing. "You know you completely exasperate me, right?"

"Can't say I'm surprised. I think I have that effect on most people I meet."

At least she was responding with a bit of morbid humor. He got it. Most people in law enforcement used sarcasm or bad humor in order to deal with what they had to live with on a daily basis. Heidi had been around long enough to adopt the technique.

He groaned. "Fine."

A hand on his arm pulled his attention from her to his grandfather. "Gramps?"

"More trouble for the pretty reporter, huh?" While the older man looked steady as a rock, his brows were drawn tight and a muscle in his jaw pulsed, revealing his tight hold on his anger and fear.

"No kidding," Nick told him.

From the corner of his eye, Nick spotted John Robinson heading straight for Heidi. Knowing she was in no condition to deal with her colleague, he nudged his grandfather. "Can you head that guy off at the pass? He and Heidi don't get along, and she may deck him if he says something snarky."

With a gleam in his eyes, his grandfather nodded. "My pleasure."

Turning, Nick found Heidi staring at him. She blinked. "Thanks."

"You're welcome. Now, let's give your statement and get some food. I have a feeling we're going to need it."

SIX

When Heidi was done giving her statement to the police, it was two o'clock in the afternoon.

She was conscious that Nick was right by her side through the whole thing. All of it. He held her hand while she spoke to the MPs. He kept his hand on her shoulder when he encouraged her to let the paramedic check her out. And, finally, he took her to the newspaper office and sat patiently in the corner of her cubicle while she typed up the story for Lou.

"Wow, you just can't stay out of trouble, can you?"

Heidi paused and then lifted her head to find John Robinson hovering just outside her cubicle. Nick looked up from the magazine he'd been reading and set it aside.

"Not in the mood, John," Heidi said and turned her attention back to her computer.

"A shoot-out is a pretty big deal. How did that guy get a semiautomatic on the base, anyway?"

"I think that the MPs are probably working on that," she said.

"Really? And you were the one who saw the guy run out of the training center, too. As well as get chased by a gun-wielding maniac outside your home."

"He didn't chase us. We chased him." She paused, looked up. "What are you implying?"

"I'm not implying anything. I'm just saying it's kind of odd, isn't it?"

"Spit it out, Robinson," Nick said.

"Fine." He jabbed a finger at Heidi. "I think you want to work on the Red Rose Killer so bad that you're setting up these little incidents to make Lou think you're the better reporter. Kind of like a daredevil reporter who'll go after any story no matter what."

Heidi stared at him for a good three seconds, then rose. "Get out."

"You're not going to deny it?"

"No, I'm not. You've made up your mind, and your blinders wouldn't allow you to see the truth if it bit you on the nose. Now, get out of my space and leave me alone."

Robinson's nostrils flared. "You're going to get knocked off that pedestal you've put yourself on. Real soon."

"Is that a threat?" Nick asked and stepped casually in front of Heidi, partially blocking her view.

"No," Robinson said. "A promise." He spun on his heel and left.

Heidi's breath whooshed from her lungs. "What a jerk."

"Yeah. You better watch your back with that one."

She caught his gaze. "Guess I'll trust you to do that while you're watching for the other guy who's out to get me."

He huffed a short laugh. "Right." His phone rang. "I'm going to get this while you finish up."

When he returned a few minutes later, Heidi had just put the finishing touches on her piece and hit the send button. "I'm starving," she said.

"We'll grab some food on the way back to your place.

That was Westley. He said they think they've figured out how the gunman got on base."

"How?"

"Looks like he hopped a ride on a delivery truck. Security footage showed him getting out of the back when no one was watching. The weapon was in his hand. Then he tried a few cars until he found one with the keys left in it. Piecing together the footage from different cameras, it's apparent that he drove around base for a few minutes—looking for you, they think—before stopping at the church. And you know what happened after that."

"Did they catch him?"

"No. Unfortunately, he managed to get away. He ditched the car and slipped inside the Base Exchange. With the baseball cap and sunglasses, we weren't able to get a good picture of him off the security footage."

She sighed and nodded. Then stood. "All right. I think I'm ready to get out of here and get something to eat. Do you mind if we just hit the drive-through? I don't feel up to sitting in a café."

"Sure, we can do that. Let's go."

He loaded her and Annie into his SUV and they swung through a drive-through before he took her home. Once inside, he placed the food on the table.

In companionable silence, they worked together, grabbing plates and silverware, and soon, she found herself sitting across from him—albeit a bit tongue-tied. After several bites, she took a sip of soda and eyed him.

"What?" he asked before taking another bite out of his burger.

"Why are you being so nice to me?" she blurted.

He blinked. "Someone just tried to kill you. Should I be mean to you?"

She gave a low laugh. "Of course not. I don't think that would even be in your makeup. But you don't like reporters. That means you don't like me by default."

"Hmm. That's been the general feeling over the last few years."

She raised a brow. "And with me being fingered as the anonymous blogger, that should really make you think twice."

"But you're not the blogger."

"I know that, but I don't have any proof."

"I think you've proven you're not."

"Really? How's that?"

"I'm not blind, Heidi. I've been watching you, and you have integrity."

A lump gathered in her throat. "Thanks, I appreciate that. But you still don't like reporters."

"I have to admit, there's a certain reporter who might be changing my mind."

"Let me guess. John Robinson?"

He choked. Then went into coughing spasms while she pounded his back. "Are you okay?"

"I may take back my statement about liking a certain reporter. She may have integrity, but her wicked sense of humor can hurt a guy."

Heidi grinned. She couldn't help it. His expression set her heart racing. "You actually like a reporter?" She was proud of the calm, matter-of-fact tone she managed to use. "Judging by your reaction, I'm guessing it's not John."

"No, John is exactly the kind of reporter I don't like."

"So, who might it be?" Seriously? Was she *flirting* with him? The guy who hated reporters? Obviously, she was still traumatized from the day's events and was in desperate need of a good night's sleep.

Now that he had himself under control, his eyes narrowed, but a smile played around the corners of his mouth. "You really have to ask?"

Dropping her gaze to her food, she gave a small laugh even while heat crept into her cheeks. "No, I guess I don't." So. He was inclined to flirt back. Interesting.

And then the gunfire she'd escaped that morning echoed in her mind and she frowned.

His smile slipped away. "What is it?" he asked.

Swallowing the last bite of her burger, she shook her head. "This probably isn't a good idea."

"What?"

She met his eyes. "You know what. Us hanging out. Flirting a little. You being anywhere near me. That's what."

"Why not?"

"Because I might get you hurt. Someone shot at me today. Obviously, this guy is crazy and doesn't care who's in the path of his bullets."

"You were the only one in the path of those bullets. They didn't come close to anyone else."

"This time. What about next time?"

He ran a hand over his eyes. "I'm hoping there won't be a next time."

She bit her lip and nodded. "I appreciate that. But if the shooter and the bomber are one and the same, he's not going to stop."

"Then someone will have to stop *him*. Period."

The flat confidence he infused into his words gave her hope and terrified her at the same time. Because stopping him might mean putting Nick's life in danger. "Nick—"

"It's going to be okay," he said.

She shot to her feet. "Don't say that!"

His brows rose. "What? Why?"

"Because you don't know that it's going to be okay." She jabbed a finger at him. "It might *not* be okay. Sometimes, it's just *not* okay." She paced to the window and looked out through the blinds, hating that she thought to stay to the side so no one could see her. The afternoon sun shone bright—a direct contrast to her moody, overcast emotional state.

He gave a slow nod. "All right. That's true. Sometimes it's not okay."

Crossing her arms, she closed her eyes for a moment while she gathered her emotions tighter. Then she turned. "I'm sorry. It's just my dad used to tell my mom that every time he left to cover a story and she expressed concern or fear. Those were some of his last words. 'Don't worry, honey, it'll be okay,' he said. Well, trust me, it wasn't okay."

"Aw, Heidi, I'm so sorry." Nick rose and stepped over to her, the look of sheer compassion in his eyes making her want to cry all over again.

But she refused. That wouldn't help anything. She set her chin. "Don't worry about it. I shouldn't have reacted so strongly."

"But some things do turn out okay, right?"

She sniffed and offered him a small smile. "Yes, some things do. Specific things. Like the fact that I'm still alive. And I have you watching out for me. That's definitely okay."

"Good," he said softly. "Because I'm glad you're still alive and I'm for sure watching out for you."

"Thank you. I appreciate it." She sighed. "And now, I need to work."

"Anything I can help you with?"

"Not unless you want to give me the scoop on the evidence you found at the training center."

"Sorry, that's a negative."

Letting her shoulders droop, she nodded. "I kind of figured."

He sighed. "Heidi, it doesn't have anything to do with whether or not I trust you. It's an investigation. There are some things I simply can't talk about."

"I know." She smiled. "It's okay."

When his brow lifted at her use of the words, she shrugged. "You can say those words when it really is— or is going to be—okay. Just don't say them when you have no way of knowing if it's going to be okay or not. You can't predict the future."

"Got it." He cleared his throat, stepped back and started cleaning up the remains of their lunch. "I'll let you do what you need to do. Work, take a nap and recover, or whatever. Just do me a favor?"

"What?"

"Don't go anywhere alone. Don't make yourself a target. Stay inside and stay safe."

Her jaw tightened at the request. "I won't be a prisoner in my own home."

"Don't look at it as a prison. Look at it as a safe house."

She rolled her eyes. "Nick—"

"Please." He placed his hands on her shoulders. "I don't want to see you get hurt—or worse."

The look of compassion in his eyes had morphed into something entirely different. "Why do you care so much?" she whispered.

"I don't know." He gave a low laugh. "A few days ago, I would have said you were as irritating as a gnat."

"Well, thanks. And now?"

"Now that I'm getting to know you a bit more…well, let's just say I want to continue to be able to do that."

She swallowed. Hard. "Okay."

"So, are you going to be all right if I leave you here alone? And be honest with me. Today was really scary. It's only natural that you might not want to be alone."

"Are you a counselor now?" she teased half-heartedly.

His lips turned up in a sad-tinged smile. "Just a guy who's been through some scary stuff."

She nodded. "I think I'll be all right. I've got coverage on my home, remember?" With a sigh, he stepped over to her and wrapped her in a hug. "I like you, Heidi Jenks."

The thud-thud-thudding of her own heart said she liked him, too.

He pressed a kiss to her forehead and she blinked.

"Call me if you need anything," he said. "Promise?"

Still reeling from the feel of his lips on her skin, she simply nodded.

And then he was gone.

And she was alone…

…with the fact that someone wanted her dead. And she was falling in love with Nick Donovan. She wasn't sure which scared her more.

Nick gave himself a mental slap. He was doing it again. Letting his heart have a say in how he acted. He decided he needed some rules when it came to Heidi.

Rule number one: keep your distance. Emotionally and physically. Which led to rule number two.

Rule number two: stay at arm's length—i.e. not close enough to hug.

Rule number three: definitely no hugging.

New rule number four: no kissing of foreheads.

Seriously, he had to get it together.

He let himself into his home and found his grandfather in the recliner, watching football. "Gramps? What are you doing here? Thought you were golfing."

His grandfather muted the game. "After everything settled down, the others decided to postpone and try again next week. I'm on the schedule. How's your girl?"

"My girl?"

A raised eyebrow was the only response from Gramps. Nick resisted rolling his eyes. "She's fine. For now."

"Why was someone shooting at her?"

"We think it's the person who bombed the training center. She was there when it happened and saw a guy in a ski mask and hoodie running from the place just before the explosion. The guy didn't realize she was there and took off his ski mask. Then saw Heidi."

"That would explain it."

"Only the hoodie hid his face enough that she was only able to give a partial description. Good enough for a detailed drawing of a guy wearing a hoodie, but nothing more than that."

"Frustrating."

"No kidding."

"So what are you doing back here? You should be watching out for her."

"She's got someone on her place."

"Then what are you going to do?"

"What do you mean?"

"You're standing there, with your keys in your hand and that look in your eyes."

"What look?"

Another raised brow. Nick huffed a short laugh. His grandfather could read him so well.

"I think I'm going to talk to Justin Blackwood and

see if he thinks any of this is related to our ongoing investigation of Boyd Sullivan."

"It's Sunday. Supposed to be a day of rest."

"Unfortunately, killers don't seem to care about that. Which makes it hard for the good guys to take the day off."

"I know, boy. I've been there. Just don't like to see you working so hard."

"Wish I didn't have to, but at least I like what I do." He did like his job. He might wish it wasn't necessary, but as long as there were bad guys with bombs, he would do his best to stop them.

He shot a text to Justin, who answered that he was in the conference room of the base command office. The captain agreed to meet and Nick headed back out the door. "Sorry I can't stay and watch the game with you."

"Trust me, you're not missing anything. The Cowboys are playing like they've never seen a football. It's maddening."

Nick gave a low laugh and headed for his truck.

When he pulled into the parking lot of the base command building, he noted several other vehicles he recognized.

Inside, he made his way to the conference room, where he found Justin with Westley, Oliver and Ava. Files were spread across the table and yellow legal pads held copious notes. "Did my invitation get lost in the mail?"

Justin waved him to a seat. "You didn't miss anything. I knew you were with Heidi." He met Nick's gaze. "Is she all right?"

"She is. She's at home resting. Or working. Probably the latter. There's an officer on her house, watching out for her."

"Okay, good." Justin caught him up on what the quartet had been discussing. "Vanessa's been keeping an eye on Yvette but hasn't seen any indication that Yvette is hiding anything or is in contact with Sullivan, but it's only been twenty-four hours. We're going to keep up with the surveillance."

"That sounds wise. If Boyd had anything to do with that explosion, he could be lying low for a bit until the investigation slows."

Justin nodded. "The good thing is, Sullivan's targets have received no more threats. We've got those who've received roses under protection and there've been no movements against them. Heidi still needs protection, though, so we'll keep someone on her."

"Which brings me to a question," Nick said. "Do you think Sullivan is behind the threats to Heidi?"

"I don't know. If Sullivan had a hand in blowing up the training center, then I'd say it's possible. But until we find the bomber, I don't think we can make that assumption."

"So, in the case of the others, Sullivan's biding his time," Nick said. "Waiting."

"That's what I think. He sure hasn't decided to stop."

Nick shook his head. "This shouldn't be taking so long. Why is it so hard to catch him?"

"We've all been asking ourselves that question," Oliver said.

Ava shrugged. "He's smart."

"And rubbing our faces in the fact that he's smarter," Westley muttered.

"He'll mess up," Justin said.

"Right," Nick said, "hopefully before someone else dies."

His phone rang, and Heidi's number flashed at him.

"Excuse me while I get this." He slipped into the hall-way. "Heidi? Everything okay?"

"I need a favor, if you don't mind."

"What's that?"

"I'm going to do a couple of interviews. MP Evan Hendrix is going with me so I should be fine, but could you pick me up when I'm finished?"

"Yes, of course. Wait a minute. What interviews?"

"For the medals, Nick."

"And you have to leave your house? Can't you just do phone interviews?"

A sigh reached him. "I could, I suppose, but it's really hard to read body language over the phone."

"FaceTime? Skype?"

"Nick, this is my job. I promise to be careful. I'll take every precaution and I'll have Evan with me."

"I still don't like it."

"Sorry. Talk to you later. I'll text you my location, if you can come get me."

"I'll be there." Oh, yes, he'd be there. Because while Evan was very likely a good soldier, there was no way he'd watch out for Heidi like Nick would. And he was going to make sure this type of situation didn't crop up in the future.

Heidi glanced at her watch and pressed a hand against her rumbling stomach as she left the last interview for the day. She'd texted Nick her location and told him Evan needed to leave but would wait with her until Nick arrived.

And true to his word, he stayed as close as a burr.

They walked down the steps of the latest theft victim's home and Heidi placed the recorder in her pocket.

"You're good at that," Evan said.

"Thanks."

"Seriously. You asked great questions, were compassionate about her loss, and didn't lead her to answers that you wanted her to have. You let her come up with her own. I've seen a lot of reporters, even answered some of their questions, but I've never seen one do it the way you do."

Heidi gave him a smile. "That's really kind of you to say so. Unfortunately, not everyone in the business acts with integrity." Understatement of the year? "But my dad taught me that integrity comes before the story. And that if I act in such a way, I'll always be the better reporter—and others will trust me." A flash of grief speared her. "And while it takes years to build relationships and gain the trust of others, lies can destroy that in seconds."

"You're referring to the fact that people think you're the anonymous blogger."

"Yes."

"Do you know why they think that?"

"I suspect because John Robinson spread that rumor." She sighed. "You know, I get that he's ambitious. This job is very competitive and cutthroat and it can bring out the worst in people." She met his gaze. "But it doesn't have to be that way. I want to help catch the bad guys, not tell them what's going on in an investigation by leaking stuff that will help them." She shook her head. "But I don't know how to prove to everyone that I'm not the blogger. Other than to continue doing my job with integrity and honesty." She shrugged. "And hope, in the end, that pays off and people see it."

"After hanging out with you and watching you work, I don't believe you're the blogger."

She squeezed his hand. "Thank you, I appreciate that. Now, pass the word, will you?"

He laughed. "Sure."

Nick pulled to the curb and stepped out. "Sorry it took me so long." He walked around and opened the door for her, a scowl on his face.

"No problem. Evan kept me company." She said her goodbyes to the MP and climbed into the passenger seat of Nick's work truck. She buckled her seat belt and scratched Annie's head while watching her ill-tempered chauffeur settle into the driver's seat. "Are you okay, Nick?"

He shot her a frown. "I'm fine."

"Then why are your eyes narrowed, brow furrowed and smoke curling from your nose?"

"Smoke?"

"Might as well be. What's the problem? Did something happen with the case?"

A sigh slipped from him and the frown faded a bit. "Nothing."

"Nothing's wrong or there's nothing more with the case?"

"Both."

"Liar. Maybe not about the case, but something's definitely wrong about you. What is it?"

"I didn't—" The scowl deepened. "Never mind. It's not important."

She let it slide while a fragment of hurt lodged in her heart. "Fine." Once thing she'd learned about Nick—if he wasn't going to talk, he wasn't going to talk.

Silence dropped between them.

"What are you going to do now?" he finally said as he turned onto Canyon Boulevard.

"Go home and write this story."

"What did the victim have to say about the robbery?"

"The same as all the others. She was out to dinner with her family. When she came home, her house had been ransacked and the medals were missing from a box in the top of her closet. Along with three hundred dollars in cash."

"Doesn't anyone use safes anymore?"

She huffed a laugh. "Guess not."

He pulled to a stop in her driveway. "Thanks for being smart."

Hand on the door handle, she paused. "What do you mean?"

"You called me. You took precautions."

With a sigh she turned back to him. "Of course. I'm not stupid."

"I didn't mean to imply you were. It's just that I guess I didn't expect that. I would have thought you were the type to get a lead on a story and just take off regardless of the consequences. That if you needed to conduct an interview you would just do it without thinking things through."

"Remember the fact that someone tried to kill me today?" She stepped out of the vehicle. "Thanks, Nick. I really appreciate that you think so highly of me. Go home. And don't come back until you can get over your preconceived notions of who I am and are willing to take the time to find out." She stared at him, fighting tears. "Because you really don't have a clue." She slammed the car door.

And then she ran for her home. Once inside, she leaned against the door and placed a hand over her pounding heart. A heart that was more and more drawn to the man who'd just hurt her feelings in a major way. She was so on the emotional roller coaster when she was in Nick's presence. The thought that they might never really get along or move forward into some kind of romantic relationship because of her job pained her.

She sighed and moved into the den. And stopped. Wait a minute. Something was off. She took in the sofa, the recliner, the end tables. What was it? Everything looked fine…except for the throw on the back of the chair by the fireplace. When had she put that there? She kept it on the couch.

Had Nick moved it when he'd been here last? Pressing a hand against her forehead, she couldn't remember. Uneasiness settled in her gut. Had someone been in her home?

Nick slammed a fist on the wheel and Annie whined. He glanced at the animal, and her sad eyes drilled him. If he didn't know better, he'd almost believe she was chastising him for being a jerk.

He sighed. He *had* been a jerk. A colossal one. What had compelled him to say such a thing to her?

Fear.

The answer leaped into his mind. He shoved it away before snatching it back. Fear? Yes. Because if he gave her the power, she could hurt him.

Not to mention the fact that someone was out to kill her.

What if that person actually succeeded?

And he'd pushed her away. Made her run from him. Jerk.

His phone rang and instead of opening the door and going after Heidi, he lifted the device to his ear. "What?"

"Having a good day, I see?"

Justin's voice made him wince and clear his throat. "Sorry."

"Have you seen the latest blog post?"

"No. Why?"

"It claims the bombing of the training center is being linked back to Boyd Sullivan."

"What? We haven't said that officially. It's just been speculated about. How would they know that?" He slapped the wheel again.

"Just like all the other information this person is managing to get her hands on."

"It's not Heidi."

The line fell quiet. Then Justin cleared his throat. "Are you sure about that?"

Was he? Completely one hundred percent sure? "Yes, I'm sure. As sure as a gut feeling can be."

"Sometimes a gut feeling is better than any evidence," Justin said. "All right. We'll keep looking. Not that Heidi won't still be in the pool of suspects, but—"

The explosion rocked his car, throwing him into the passenger seat. The windshield shattered, raining shards of hard glass down on him.

Ears ringing, he lifted himself up to squint against the flames shooting from Heidi's front window.

SEVEN

Nick pulled himself out of his SUV and let a barking Annie out of her area. Keeping the leash around his wrist, he stumbled toward the house only to fall back when the heat scorched him. "Heidi!"

Sirens were already screaming. Westley and Felicity hurried down their front porch. Westley reached him first and gripped his forearm. "Nick! Are you okay? You're bleeding."

"Heidi's in there!" Horror clawed at him. His lungs tightened against the smoke and the fear. There was no way she could have survived that.

Westley went white and Felicity cried out, covering her mouth with her hand. "No," she whispered. "I don't believe it."

There had to be a way in, a way to save her. Nick raced through the narrow pathway between her house and Felicity's, rounded the corner and stopped. The fence. He'd forgotten about the fence. Scrambling for a way to climb over, he paused.

A noise caught his attention even over the sirens and the roar of the burning home. A cry? A cough?

He followed the fence line and turned to see Heidi sitting outside the fence, staring at her home.

"Heidi!"

She looked up at his call, her face streaked with tears and dirt. He raced over to her and dropped to his knees. Gripping her upper arms, he took in the sight of her, looking for any outward signs of trauma. "Are you all right?"

"No!" She swiped a hand across her cheek, smearing the dirt. She pointed. "Look what he did! Just look! It's gone. All of it." He pulled her to him and she buried her forehead against his chest. Annie whined and tried to shove her face between them. Then she licked Heidi's ear. Sobs broke through and Heidi hugged him tighter and let him hold her.

"Heidi! Nick!"

Westley's harsh cry pulled Nick's attention to the man who'd followed the same path Nick had taken just minutes before. He hurried over to them. "Heidi! Boy, am I glad to see you."

She sniffed and hiccupped, but didn't move from Nick's hold.

"What were you doing out here? Because whatever it was, it saved your life."

She giggled, and Nick frowned. Was she going to get hysterical on him? She said something and he missed it. "What?" She pointed and he followed her finger to a white trash bag lying on the ground. "Heidi?"

"The trash," she said. "I was taking the trash out." Another slightly hysterical giggle. "Taking out the trash—a chore I hate with everything in me and put off until the last possible moment—saved my life. I'll never complain about *that* again." She dissolved into another fit of giggles, followed quickly by gasping sobs. Nick simply held her while her home burned.

His gaze met Westley's. "We have to stop this guy."

"I pulled security footage from the night of the training center explosion and saw the man she saw, but there's no way to tell who he was. By the time Heidi said he pulled the ski mask off and turned, he was out of range of the camera. So far, we've gotten no leads on the sketch Carl worked up."

Heidi had stopped crying and he figured by her still-ness she was listening. "He pulled the mask off because he knew it was safe to do so. He knows this base. First we need to investigate every single person who lives on this base."

Westley sighed, but nodded. "That's what I was thinking. I'm also thinking it's going to take a while."

"Then we might as well get started."

Heidi sat in the back of the ambulance next to Nick, who hadn't let her out of his sight. The paramedic had checked her out, then cleaned and bandaged several cuts on his face, arms and hands.

"They're not deep, but your face didn't like the force the glass came with," the medic said.

"I know. It's fine."

"No head trauma that I can see on either of you, so you can count your blessings for that."

"I'm alive," Heidi said, "I'm grateful." But the loss hurt. She wouldn't put on a brave face and pretend it didn't. Her notes, her laptop, her files. Everything. Gone. Either to the explosion and fire or water damage. The only reason she wasn't in a puddle on the floor of the ambulance was because she had almost everything backed up to the cloud. The only thing she might not be able to access was the latest piece she'd been writing. Unable to remember if she'd saved it to her online backup, Heidi gave a mental shrug. She could rewrite it.

A flash to her right cause her to recoil. She blinked and finally focused her gaze on John Robinson lowering his camera. "Really?" she demanded.

He shrugged. "I just follow the stories."

"Right." She wouldn't get into it with him. One, it seemed to spur him to be even more obnoxious, and two, she simply didn't have the energy.

Nick stepped out of the ambulance and stood in front of the doorway so Robinson couldn't see into the back where Heidi was. "Get away from here. Now."

His low command sent Robinson stumbling backward. Heidi leaned to the right to see fear flash in the man's eyes, but his chin was raised. "You have no right to stop me from getting my story."

"You have no right to impede medical treatment."

With a roll of his eyes, Robinson left. "I got my picture. I guess that's all I need. I'd love a statement from the victim, but I'm assuming that's not going to happen."

He had that right. "Thanks, John. I appreciate your concern." She couldn't help it. His lack of professionalism infuriated her. No story was worth sacrificing the human touch, expressing sympathy to one's fellow man. Reporters like him made reporters like her look bad. And she just plain didn't like it.

"I can see the smoke coming out of your ears," Nick said to her when Robinson left, "and it has nothing to do with your house blowing up."

She scowled. "That man gets under my skin. Way under. I've got to find a way to let him and his actions roll off my back."

"Be a duck."

"What?"

"Your new mantra when it comes to Robinson."

"Oh. Be a duck. Meaning let the irritation I feel for the man roll off?"

"Exactly. Come on," he said. "Forget about Robinson. We've got to get you settled somewhere."

"I guess I'll have to find a hotel."

He frowned. "No way. Not when you have friends."

"I do have a few friends, but I'm not going to put any of them in danger. Not when this guy is going around blowing up houses."

Felicity pushed her way through the gathering crowd. "Heidi!" She rushed forward and hugged her, forcing Nick to drop her hand and step back. "I'm so glad you're okay," Felicity said. "At first, I thought you'd... that you'd...that you were—"

"That I was in the house when it blew?"

"Yes." Another tight hug. "I'm so glad you're all right."

"Thank you." Heidi looked back at the smoldering structure. "At least it was just mostly the front of the house that took the brunt of the blast. It wasn't big enough to take the whole thing down. Or cause damage to yours."

"I'm just glad you weren't hurt." Felicity squeezed her hands, then let her go. "What can I do to help?" She bit her lip. "You'll need a place to stay."

"She can stay with me and my grandfather," Nick said.

Heidi blinked and her mouth rounded as she processed his words. "What?"

"We have a guest bedroom, and the colonel is there most of the time. And he obviously knows how to use a gun so you'd have built-in protection."

"But I—"

"That sounds like the perfect solution," Felicity said. "I'll run back to my place and grab you some clothes to wear. I'm going to assume all your uniforms are gone?"

"Except the two at the cleaners, you."

Annie whined at his side and Nick stroked her ears. "We'll get to work on this one soon, girl." He looked up at Heidi. "We've got to wait for clearance from the fire department, then we'll go in."

Justin Blackwood climbed out of his official vehicle and approached. "Anyone hurt?"

"No, but not because someone wasn't trying," Nick answered for her. Surprisingly, Heidi didn't care. The two of them talked while she rubbed her still-ringing ears. She just wanted to leave, to be alone and process all that had happened.

After some questions, she finally got her wish and Nick led her and Annie to his vehicle. "Stay here for now. I'm going to get the colonel to come take us to my house." He squeezed her hand and called his grandfather. From the quickness of the call, she assumed the man hadn't asked any questions. "He'll be right here." He glanced at his vehicle. "Thankfully, I was in my work truck. It'll be impounded for evidence. I'll be back with Annie to see if we can determine what caused the blast. Meanwhile I'm sure Justin will check out each camera within a mile of your home and see if there's anyone suspicious."

Three minutes later the colonel pulled to a stop just beyond the scene. He stepped out of his sedan and took in the sight with a shake of his head and concern in his eyes. "Are you two all right?" he asked as he approached them.

"We're fine, Gramps. Just need a ride home."

"Come on, then."

Once at the men's home, Colonel Hicks led the way up the front porch steps and into the foyer. Nick shut the door behind them.

"You're welcome to stay here as long as you need," the colonel told her.

"Thank you, sir."

"Nick can show you where to stow your gear. I'll get the bathroom ready for you."

She followed Nick to the guest room and stepped inside to see a twin bed against the far wall, a dresser next to the door and a comfortable chair under the window.

"The bathroom is just outside the room, off the hall," Nick said. "In the second drawer, you'll find toiletries. We keep them for visiting family and friends. Help yourself to anything you need."

"Towels and washcloths are by the sink," the colonel said from behind Nick.

"Thank you very much."

The colonel led the way back to the kitchen, where he gestured for her to sit. "Coffee?"

"Decaf?"

He laughed. "Of course. Even that keeps me up at night sometimes, though."

With the mug in front of her, she wrapped her hands around the warm porcelain and took a deep breath. Someone had just tried to kill her. And almost succeeded. The thought almost didn't compute. "How did someone get a bomb in my house?" she asked.

"Probably picked a time when no one was watching it," Nick said with a sigh. "If you weren't there, there was no reason to have someone on your home—or so we thought."

"Of course."

His phone buzzed and he glanced at the screen. "Looks like it's time for Annie and me to go to work." He called for the dog and she rose from her spot by the fireplace to pad into the kitchen. "You ready to go catch some bad guys, girl?"

Her tail wagged, and he slipped her into the harness hanging near the door. Then he added booties to protect her paws. He looked over his shoulder at Heidi and his grandfather as he slung his pack over his back. "You two lie low. I'll be back soon."

Nick arrived at Heidi's home to find the place roped off and the crime scene unit working in an organized grid. He showed his ID to the officer in charge and was allowed to pass under the tape.

Annie trotted at his side. Justin was still on the scene and Nick made his way over to him and Westley.

"Glad you're here," Justin said. "Let us know what you and Annie find."

Even though firefighters had put the fire out, just like with the training center, he and Annie started examining the debris farther away from the hot areas. While they worked, Nick thought. What was the best way to catch the guy who wanted to wipe Heidi off the planet? Because failing to do so wasn't an option.

Footsteps behind him caught his attention and he turned to see Westley.

"Find anything, Nick?"

"Some scraps that Annie found interesting. She was most interested in the den area. Looks like he hid a bomb, possibly dynamite or C-4, in the den area. We'll see what the lab says."

"ATF is here once again. Didn't even have to use the GPS this time. We've got to stop this guy."

Probably hadn't had to use it the last time, either. But Nick got the point. Two explosions on base were two too many. "My thoughts exactly."

"Security Forces are going crazy scanning video footage of the training center explosion. And now this." He gave a disgusted sigh and shook his head. "I'll leave you to it. Let me know what you find."

"Of course."

The man left and Nick and Annie went back to work. Once the place cooled down, he and Annie and the ATF investigators would go inside and see if they could find what triggered the explosion. When they had some of the materials, they would be able to compare it to the training center evidence.

However, Nick was pretty sure he knew exactly who the bomber was. It had to be the guy from the training center. He was scared Heidi could ID him and he was going all out to make sure she didn't. He was a guy who wanted Heidi dead and he had to be stopped before he succeeded in getting what he wanted.

EIGHT

Heidi sat curled up in the large chair next to the fireplace and sipped her second cup of decaf coffee. Her eyes had grown heavy as the hours passed. The colonel had finally declared he was headed to bed. The weapon in his hand made her wonder, but she hadn't argued. She wanted the time alone to think. And she'd had that. Now she was tired of thinking and just wanted to go to bed.

But her mind wouldn't let her.

The fact that Nick wasn't back kept her glued to the chair.

Minutes later she heard footsteps on the front porch, followed by voices. She walked to the window to look out.

"…might be back on base," Justin said.

"When did you learn that?"

"Just now. When we were finishing up at Heidi's house, Vanessa Gomez reported that someone was watching her house. When MPs arrived, the person ran."

"Vanessa got a rose from Sullivan. You think he's back to make good on his threat?"

"I do. I don't have proof, though, so keep this under your hat."

"Of course."

"I was on the way home and figured I'd stop by and

let you know. Anyway, get some rest. I'll see you to-morrow."

"Thanks."

The door opened and Heidi stumbled back. Nick raised a brow, then frowned. He stepped inside and narrowed his eyes. "Guess you heard that?"

"Um…yes. I guess I did. But I wasn't eavesdropping on purpose. I heard voices and looked out the window."

He sighed. "That's not to go in the paper, under-stand? We don't need to cause a panic on base until we have more information."

"But you think Sullivan's back."

"There's evidence to indicate he is. Yes."

"Nick, people have to know. They have to be on guard."

"And we're going to let them know. As soon as we're positive. So, please. Nothing in the paper about it until we're sure."

"But you'll let me have the exclusive?"

"Sure."

She nodded. "Okay."

"You wouldn't have printed it, anyway, would you?"

"No, but I figure it doesn't hurt to weasel the exclu-sive." She took a sip from the mug. "So, how did it go at my house? What's left of it, anyway."

He sighed. "Annie did a good job as always. There weren't any other explosives to be found and we scooped up some evidence that the lab will examine. Now she's back at the kennel getting some much-deserved rest."

"Good, I'm glad." She stood and began to pace.

"Heidi, what's going through that head of yours?"

She stopped and faced him. "Who am I, Nick?"

"What do you mean?"

"I mean, tonight, just about everything I've worked

for has been destroyed. Sure, all my files are safe, but I've been thinking. What if they weren't?"

He took her hand and pulled her over to sit on the sofa, then planted himself opposite her. "I'm not following."

Palming her eyes, she fell silent, then lowered her hands and looked up. "I guess what I'm trying to say is, if I can't do my job—and right now, that's looking pretty iffy—then who am I?"

"You're still you. First Lieutenant Heidi Jenks. And not being able to do your job is just a temporary problem. As soon as we catch this guy, you're back to being a star reporter."

She sighed. "I've never been a star reporter." She shrugged at his frown. "Yes, I'm good at my job. Yes, I can write an excellent article. And yes, I can be like a bulldog with a bone. But I'm not cutthroat. I won't step on someone else to get to that next rung on the reporting ladder. So...what does that make me?"

"Admirable," he whispered.

"But John Robinson," she said as though he hadn't spoken, "now, there's a man who'll go behind your back and do whatever it takes to get a story. No matter the consequences or the fallout."

"He's a jerk."

"Yes, he is. But he also gets the job done. So, is that what I need to be? A jerk?"

"No." He clasped her hand. "Please don't even go there."

She sighed and blinked. "I'm sorry. I'm thinking out loud." She paused. "You don't think Robinson hates me enough to blow up my house, do you? You don't think he would be so desperate to keep me out of the loop on not only the training center bombing, but the Red

Rose Killer story, that he'd do something like this to throw me off?"

Nick threaded his fingers around hers. "I don't know, but you shouldn't jump to conclusions until you talk to him. Does he even have any experience handling explosives?"

His touch grounded her. Centered her. Made her very aware of him. "As far as I know, he doesn't have any background dealing with explosives. Then again, I guess if someone's desperate enough, it's not hard to find out what you need to know. He's been awfully territorial. I mean, you saw him at church—and then after my house blew up. He'll do anything to get a story. I think I need to talk to him."

"Look, Heidi, you're a good reporter with good instincts. But don't let your emotions start getting in the way. Get the facts before you act."

Heidi drew in a deep breath. "Of course. You're right."

"Why don't you get a good night's sleep and we'll take care of whatever needs to be taken care of in the morning? For now, I think you need to relax and take some time to regroup."

She nodded. "I think that's a good idea."

He stood and pulled her up. For a moment, she simply stared into his eyes, thought he might say something else, but then he cleared his throat and took a step back. "Good night, Heidi."

"Good night, Nick."

In her bedroom, she drew in a deep breath. Somehow she'd ignored the spark of attraction that had flared when she'd stood in front of him in the living room. She had other things that needed her focus. Not chasing a romance with a man who was so gun-shy around reporters. She pulled her small recorder from her pocket and spoke in detail the conversation she'd overheard. Then with more reluctance than bravado, she grabbed her phone and dialed John's number.

"Hello? Robinson here."

"Did you blow up my house?"

"Did I what? Heidi? What are you talking about?"

"Did you blow up my house? Are you so threatened by me that you want to get rid of me? To kill me?"

For a moment silence echoed back at her. "You're a piece of work, Heidi. I know we're rivals, but for you to accuse me of that is really low. Especially for you."

He sounded so sincere that guilt immediately flooded her. She swallowed. "I'm…I'm sorry, John. I didn't want to ask. I just figure I need to cover all my bases."

"Well, you don't have to worry about me being the one trying to kill you." He gave a short huff. "I'll admit to being willing to profit from all the trouble you're having, but I'm not the one instigating it."

"Wow. Thanks."

"Hey, it's just the way it is." He paused. "But no, I'm not trying to kill you."

"Well, I appreciate that. I'm…sorry I practically accused you of doing so. I know how false accusations can hurt."

"Exactly." He paused. "You wouldn't want to give me an interview, would you?"

She laughed. "Good night, Robinson. I'll see you around."

So, if it wasn't John, it had to be the guy she'd seen at the training center. She picked up the recorder and worked out her thoughts on the machine. It always helped to go back and listen and make sure she hadn't forgotten anything when she worked on a piece.

A light knock interrupted her. She opened the door to find Nick standing there, a speculative gleam in his eyes. She raised a brow. "What?"

He set a glass of water and some ibuprofen on her dresser. "Just in case."

"Ah. Yes, that's a good idea. Thanks."

"Night again."

"Night."

He turned, paused and turned back. "Heidi?"

"Yes?"

"I couldn't help overhearing your apology to Robinson."

She flushed. "I suppose you think I should have waited to confront him in person."

"I don't think it matters. Were you wrong? You don't think he was involved in blowing up your home?"

"It sure sounded like that on the phone. I wouldn't mind having concrete proof, but if I were to go with my gut, I'd say he wasn't involved."

"And you apologized."

"Of course. I try to do that when I make a mistake."

He shook his head. "If I hadn't seen it, I don't know that I would have believed it."

She rolled her eyes. "Thanks."

"No, I need to be thanking you. It was refreshing. I needed to see that—as a reminder that everyone is different and deserves to be judged based on who they are, not based on preconceived notions. Like you said in the car before you slammed the door in my face." She winced and he smiled. "I deserved it."

"Sorry about that. I kind of lost my temper a bit."

"I understand." He drew in a deep breath. "Anyway, thanks. Say, I figure you have tomorrow off since I doubt anyone is going to expect you to work after losing your home. Would you like me to take you into town to shop for some things?"

"I was going to ask Felicity if she wanted to go with me, but I know she has to work tomorrow."

"So, is that a yes?"

She nodded. "It is if it won't inconvenience you any."

"It won't. Maybe getting off the base will help."

She frowned. "Do you think it's safe?"

"As safe as staying here."

"That's not a very good argument."

"True. I'll watch out for you. We can watch each other's backs."

"All right, sounds good."

"Perfect. Good night."

He left and she carried the water and medicine to the end table. She shut the door and got ready for bed, feeling safe in the home of the man who seemed to want to hold her at arm's length and pull her close—all at the same time. She sighed and decided not to get too comfortable. As she'd learned the hard way, feeling safe didn't mean she was.

Nick took a sip of the coffee his grandfather had made and thought about what he'd accidentally overheard. Heidi had actually apologized to Robinson. Since when did reporters apologize? Especially ones who were as competitive as those two. He had a feeling if the shoe was on the other foot, Robinson wouldn't have had the gumption to do the same as Heidi. The reporter who'd covered his mother's death sure hadn't. But Heidi had. To someone she didn't even like, no less.

Nick had to admit, it said a lot about her character. She hadn't known he was listening—albeit unintentionally. When he'd realized she was on the phone, he'd started to walk away, but stopped when he heard her say Robinson's name. He'd been ready to offer his comfort if Robinson lit into her, but it had sounded as if they'd had a civil conversation. Not exactly friendly, but at least she hadn't become upset and hadn't needed his intervention. A strong woman, she could take care of herself.

Except when someone was blowing up her house.

"You okay, son?"

His grandfather stood in the doorway, dressed in his pajamas and long robe with matching slippers. "I'm okay. You look dapper."

"Have to dress a little better when we have company."

"We don't have company often."

"Exactly. Now, what's eating at you?"

Nick raised a brow. "What do you think?"

Gramps laughed. "Yeah, I thought so."

"I don't know what to do about her."

"Take it one day at a time."

"Hmm." He sighed. "I have to admit that I'm worried someone's going to succeed in killing her before I find who it is."

His grandfather slipped into the chair next to him. "I would say that's a real problem."

He met the older man's eyes. "How do I take care of her, Gramps?"

"Don't know what else you can do short of taking her off base and hiding her away somewhere."

"An idea I've thought of, but doubt she'll go for." He paused. "She's getting to me."

"I know."

Of course he did. "I overheard her apologize to someone just now. A reporter. Apologizing. It struck me."

"Right in the heart?"

"Something like that."

"You've wanted an apology from a reporter ever since your mother died and they printed that ridiculous story."

"I guess you're right. And hearing hers…well, I think it just healed something deep inside me."

"You need to tell her that."

Nick smiled. "I will."

His grandfather stood and bid him good-night, then disappeared down the hall to his bedroom.

Sitting at the table in the quiet with only a soft glow coming from the light over the sink, Nick considered the next steps in the investigation. They'd confirmed the training center explosion was deliberate. Residue identified it as C-4. Easily set off with a timer.

"Which explains why he was in such a hurry to get away from the training center," he muttered.

It was obvious the man in the hoodie was after Heidi and pretty determined to shut her up for good. Although, Nick had to wonder what purpose it would serve to kill her now. She'd already talked to OSI and Security Forces and told them everything.

Then again, he supposed it would help if Heidi weren't on the base to accidentally run into the man she could identify. Which, if that was the concern, meant he was on the base frequently. Or lived on it.

There'd been no word from Justin on the progress being made in checking the visitor logs, but Nick knew that was like looking for the proverbial needle in the haystack. He sighed. And running it around in his head all night wasn't going to help matters. But one thing did concern him. Did the person who wanted Heidi dead know she was staying with him and his grandfather? He couldn't help thinking about that possibility.

Nick rose and glanced out the window to see a Security Forces vehicle stationed in front of his home. He knew there was another one at the back.

He took a weapon from his safe, then stepped out onto the front porch. With a wave to the airman in the car, he started his trek around the perimeter of his home.

Nothing caught his attention. There were no moving shadows that made him jump, no mysterious sounds that he needed to investigate. All was still.

Back inside his home, he locked up, then checked all the windows. Still unable to relax—and knowing he wouldn't sleep if he tried—he kept the gun with him and stretched out on the couch, ready to defend his home and protect the woman he was growing to care about way too much.

NINE

Shopping with Nick had seemed like a good idea last night. Unfortunately, in the light of day, Heidi's indecision weighed on her, leaving her embarrassed that Nick had to see her at her worst. Indecisive and incredibly picky.

She finally stomped out of the last store, crossed the street and found a booth in the small café. He followed at a brisk trot and handed her the two bags he'd so chivalrously carried for her. "Hold on to these. I'll be right back."

Fortunately, since it was two in the afternoon, the café's busy lunchtime rush was over and only a few stragglers remained. When he returned, he set in front of her a steaming mug of hot chocolate topped with whipped cream and a caramel drizzle. He'd gotten himself the same, along with a cinnamon roll that he set in between them. "Let's eat."

She blew out a breath and couldn't help the smile that wanted to curve her lips. "Thanks. I'm sorry I'm such a lunatic when it comes to shopping. I'm just so particular and I loved my wardrobe. Before it was incinerated, anyway."

"It's okay. Shopping for clothes can be hard."

"And I don't really need that much. Not with wearing a uniform every day."

"I get it."

"And I'm not used to shopping with a guy. You make me nervous."

He slid around to sit beside her. She'd chosen a corner booth for a multitude of reasons. The most important one being it was away from windows and doors and she didn't have to worry about someone shooting her in the back. "I don't want to make you nervous," he said as he scooted closer.

She cleared her throat. "Ah. Well, that's not helping."

"Why?"

"Because you're a little close." And he smelled really, really good.

"I like being close to you," he said softly.

"You do?" The squeak those words came out on could not belong to her.

"I do. You've gotten under my skin, Heidi Jenks, and I'm really not sure what to do about it."

"I...um...hope you're not asking me for advice, because I'm really not sure what to—"

His lips cut off her words. She froze, unsure what to do. Then instinct took over and she closed her eyes, lifted her hand to cup his cheek and let the lovely sensation of being kissed by Nick Donovan wash over her.

When he lifted his head, the tender expression in his eyes was nearly her undoing. "Well, I suppose that's one thing to do when someone's under your skin," she whispered.

He grinned. Then shook his head. "Like I said, I like you, Heidi. A lot. And I'm not sure it's a good idea."

"Why? Because I'm a reporter?"

"No, you pretty much opened my eyes on that one.

I'm not worried about your motives or that you're only out for a story. I've seen your heart. You're very good at what you do and you put others first. It's obvious you care and that's why people respond so well to you."

Tears welled before she could stop them. One dripped down onto her cheek and he swiped it away with a thumb. "Thank you for that," she whispered. "I needed to hear it. I need someone to believe that I'm not the anonymous blogger and that I have integrity. I mean, *I* know it, and usually, that's enough. But this time, I think I just need others to see it, too, I guess. Which is probably stupid."

"It's not stupid," he said. "It's human."

She smiled. "I'm definitely human. With all of the shortcomings and failures that come with it, but I'm trying to rise above those, you know?"

"I know. I'm right there with you."

"You? You seem pretty perfect to me."

He let out a low chuckle. "Trust me, I'm far from perfect."

"Oh, that's right. You do have that whole distrust of reporters thing." She sighed. "But you definitely have a reason to feel that way."

"I told you. I don't feel that way about you." He leaned over and kissed her again. A light, sweet, comforting kiss that she wished could go on forever. It made her forget about the troubles surrounding her, the fear and anxiety, the despair about her lost home…everything.

When he pulled back, he enveloped her in a hug that took away what breath she had left. "I trust *you*, Heidi."

Nick listened to the words coming out of his mouth with something resembling shock. Had he just told Heidi, a reporter, that he trusted her?

Apparently. And the funny thing was, he did. He'd seen her in action. She was a go-getter and good at what she did, but she didn't step on other people or lie to get her story.

He looked down at her. "Are you all right now?"

"Yes. I'm much better. Thank you."

"Ready to do more shopping?"

She groaned and he laughed. They finished the cinnamon roll and the hot chocolate, making small talk, and Nick realized not for the first time that he could fall for this woman.

And he really shouldn't.

Why not?

Because she was a reporter.

But he trusted her, right?

Until he didn't.

"You ready to go?"

She wiped her mouth with a napkin. "Sure. I guess so."

For the next hour, they continued their shopping, with Heidi a little more relaxed and Nick a lot more conflicted. He liked Heidi. A lot. He'd been honest with that statement. And while he trusted her in the moment he told her he did, he wondered if that would last. Then he was disgusted with himself for his wishy-washy feelings. He should be able to give her the benefit of the doubt.

His gaze followed her reflection in the storefront glass as they passed a shop advertising fresh fudge. He grabbed her hand and pulled her inside.

"Whoa." She lifted her head and inhaled deeply. "Mmm. The smells in here are intoxicating."

"I have a really hard time resisting fudge—and strawberry shortcake. What's your favorite dessert?"

"Besides chocolate turtle cheesecake? Chocolate turtle fudge."

"Give me a pound of the chocolate turtle and the peanut butter cookie crunch," he told the woman behind the counter.

When he turned back to Heidi, he caught sight of a man in a hoodie just outside the shop window. He was just standing there, his face shadowed by the hood, his hands shoved into the front pockets of his jeans. Nick frowned as he pulled out his debit card and passed it to the clerk. She swiped it and handed it back to him.

He took a second to scrawl a tip and signature. When he looked back, the man was gone.

He sighed. Paranoia was not a good thing. Then again...

Picking up the bags, he nodded to the door. "Ready?"

"Sure." She unwrapped a piece of the fudge and took a bite. Then gave a piece to him.

He chewed and smiled, but his attention was on the window. "Stay behind me, okay?"

Her eyes sharpened and she frowned. "What is it?"

"I'm not sure. Maybe nothing."

"Maybe something. What?"

"A guy watching through the window. Could have been nothing, but it's making me nervous."

"You think someone followed us here?"

He shook his head. "I don't know. I was watching and didn't see anyone, but that doesn't mean someone couldn't have trailed us."

They stepped out of the shop and Nick made sure to angle himself in front of her. People walked on the sidewalk to his right and to his left. Across the street, a family sat outside at one of the tables belonging to the little café.

But he saw no man in a dark hoodie.

While he knew he hadn't imagined seeing the man, maybe he was overreacting. Nevertheless, he gripped the bags tighter with one hand and slipped his other under her elbow as they walked.

"You're making me really nervous, Nick."

"Sorry."

They made it to his car with no incident, but the whole way he felt like he had a target on his back. Or Heidi did. Once they were on the way back to the base, Nick watched the rearview mirror.

"Do you see someone?" Heidi asked him.

"Maybe. A car pulled out of the parking lot behind us." He flexed his fingers on the wheel. Then relaxed. "And it just turned off."

"I'm sorry you've gotten all caught up in this," she said softly.

"Not your fault."

"Maybe not, but I still feel bad about it. When do you think you'll hear something about the explosions? Like whether or not they're related?"

He shrugged. "Probably in the next day or so."

She fell silent and he continued to watch the road, the mirrors, the surrounding area. The shopping center wasn't too far from the base, and soon, he was turning into the entrance.

Back at his house, he helped her unload the bags and led the way inside.

He found his grandfather talking to Felicity James. She stood. "Hello, Heidi, I just stopped by to check on you."

Heidi set her bags on the end of the sofa and gave her friend a hug. "Thank you. I'm doing all right. I'm just in the process of replacing my wardrobe. I'll be sure to get your clothes washed and back to you soon."

"There's no hurry on that. Any news on who was responsible for the explosion?"

"No, not yet."

She nodded. "Well, I brought a casserole and pie for you guys for dinner. I won't stay. I just wanted to check on you."

"Thanks, Felicity, I appreciate it."

"And…"

"And what?"

"Have you seen the latest blog post?"

Heidi groaned. "Seriously? There's more?"

"Yes. Westley and Justin are fit to be tied. This anonymous blogger is causing everyone on the investigative team a lot of grief. Are you sure you don't know who it is?"

Heidi froze. "What are you saying?"

"Nothing. And I'm not accusing. I just thought maybe a name might have occurred to you, or—"

"Westley told you to come over here and ask me this, didn't he?"

A flush crept up her friend's neck and into her cheeks. She groaned. "Yes. I'm sorry."

"It's not Heidi," Nick said from behind her.

Felicity stilled, then looked past Heidi to meet Nick's eyes. "I don't think so, either."

"Then convince your husband and tell him to leave her alone. Please."

Biting her lip, Felicity gave a slow nod. "All right. I'll do my best."

"Thank you."

She rose. "Well, I guess I'll take off. Heidi, if you need anything, you'll call, right?"

"Of course. Thank you."

"No hard feelings?"

"None toward you." She scowled.

Felicity gave her a small smile, then left. Heidi's shoulders wilted. An arm slid around them. "She means well."

"I know." She sniffed. And then she followed her nose into the kitchen. "That smells amazing."

"Guess we know what we're having for dinner."

"So," the colonel said, "who's up for a game of Scrabble?"

Heidi grinned. "I love that game. And I'm good at it, too."

Nick raised a brow. "Hmm. We'll see about that."

"Is that a challenge, First Lieutenant?"

"It is, First Lieutenant."

"You're on."

It was a fun evening. They played two games and ate half the casserole and the entire apple pie before calling it a night.

On his way to his room, Nick cupped her cheek. "I'm glad you're here, Heidi." He paused. "Let me clarify. I'm not glad for the reason you needed a roof over your head, but I'm glad Gramps and I were able to provide this one."

"Thanks, Nick." He smiled, and she watched him disappear into his room before slipping into hers.

She lay in bed and stared at the ceiling. She'd enjoyed today. She'd actually had fun in a way she hadn't had in a very long time. Scrabble had been her dad's favorite game and playing tonight had resurrected memories she'd thought she'd tucked away forever. Good memories, but still painful because they brought home how much she missed her father.

But Nick's grandfather was clever and smart. He'd won the first game before Heidi had trounced them in the second. Nick had simply shaken his head and declared the tiles had been against him. "How am I supposed to come up with a word with six vowels and a *Z*? No one can win with that."

His good-natured grumbling had endeared him to her even more, and she'd been astonished at how fast the time had flown.

While she'd been granted more time off due to the explosion, Heidi planned to get back to work on the story of the stolen medals first thing in the morning.

Fatigue pulled at her and she gave in to it. Feeling safe and well guarded, Heidi let her eyes close.

Only to have them fly open after what seemed like seconds, but according to the clock, was two hours. One in the morning. What had awakened her?

She sat up and listened.

Voices.

Nothing that sounded alarming, but the reporter in her perked up. She rolled out of bed and pulled on a new pair of jeans and a lightweight sweater she'd purchased on the shopping trip with Nick.

She opened the window and the voices sharpened. "…just sitting here. I say you need to call the trainer. It's probably one of the still-missing dogs. Call Westley James. He can be here in no time."

Heidi shoved her feet into the tennis shoes next to her bed, grabbed her recorder and notebook, and hurried into the living area, where she found Nick standing in the foyer, hand on the doorknob. "I'm just going to see what's going on," he said. "You can go on back to bed."

Heidi laughed. "Right. Let's go."

"Heid—"

She slipped around him, turned the knob and was on the porch before he could blink. She thought he might have emitted a low growl, but she was more interested in what was happening over near the entrance gate. Since Nick and his grandfather lived in the end unit of the row of houses, they were closest to the gate entrance.

Which explained why she heard the commotion. With her voice-activated recorder in her pocket, notebook in hand and a protesting Nick right behind her, she hurried to see what was going on.

Nick pulled up beside her when she stopped near the growing crowd of onlookers. "What is it?" she asked the airman nearest her.

"A dog showed up."

"One of the working dogs that are still missing?" Heidi asked.

"That's what they're trying to figure out. Master Sergeant James should be here soon as well as Rusty Morton." Rusty was one of the trainers from the K-9 center.

Rusty arrived first, followed by Westley and Felicity. "What do we have here?" Westley asked.

A young airman stepped forward. He was one of the guards who monitored the base entrance gate. "Sir, I was on duty when I noticed this dog just outside the gate. He simply walked up and sat down as though waiting for someone to let him inside."

"Does he have a collar?"

"I didn't get close enough to check, sir."

Westley nodded and approached the open gate. "That looks like Patriot." The German shepherd watched him, ears up, tail wagging. "He's friendly like Patriot." Westley murmured, "Stay."

He reached for the tag and Heidi moved so she could see while describing the scene into her voice recorder. Nick stayed by her side and she thought he was looking everywhere but at the action in front of them. It hit her that he was nervous about her being out in the open.

But she was surrounded by people.

"His tag says Poco." Westley looked back at Rusty. "Call him."

"Poco! Come!" The dog's ears twitched, but he didn't move.

"Try Patriot," Westley said.

"Patriot, come!" The dog bounded over to the trainer, who scratched his ears. Rusty looked up. "This is Patriot, all right."

Other than his coat needing a good brushing, he looked healthy enough to her.

Rusty looked up. "Someone's been feeding him. Or he's found a well-stocked trash can. Not sure what made him come home, but I'm glad he's here." Westley nodded. "This gives me hope. Patriot's one of the best. One of our superstar dogs. If he found his way home, then maybe the other three will, too." He spotted Nick in the crowd and waved him over. Heidi stayed on his heels. Westley's brows rose at her presence, but she simply shot him a smile. He turned his attention to Nick. "I want to meet with the investigative team as soon as possible. We need to go house to house and see if anyone has noticed who's been taking care of this dog. Tell them his name is Poco since that's what the person would have called him."

Heidi's jaw dropped. "It's one in the morning. You're going to wake people up?"

"We do what we have to do in an investigation. You know that."

"Of course."

Zip it, Heidi.

Heidi stepped up to Westley. "Where do you think he came from?"

"I don't know. We're working on finding out."

"So, if Patriot got off the base, then did the other dogs get off, too?"

"Working on that, too. Wish I had the answers to those questions."

"And why is he wearing a different collar?" Nick asked. "Someone changed it."

"So, this guy has been missing for months and now he shows up out of the blue," Westley said. "He's on the skinny side, but not starving so he's getting food from somewhere." He ran a hand over the dog's coat. "Needs a good brushing."

"Someone's been taking care of him," Heidi said.

Westley examined the dog's paws. "And probably someone who's fairly close to the base. He didn't walk too far to get here. Paws are in fine shape."

"What's being done to find the other twenty dogs, sir? Especially the three others that Nick said were so special?" Heidi held her pen over her notebook.

"We've got people looking for them."

Heidi wasn't going to be deterred by his vague answer. "Looking where, sir?"

"Off base." He quirked a smile at her, not at all fazed by her persistence. "Is this going to be the headline in the morning?"

She shrugged. "Of course. It's news."

"Yep, I guess it is."

"Are you planning to offer a reward for the safe return of the other dogs now that you know it's possible they could be nearby?" she asked.

"We were hoping it wouldn't come to that, but it's possible we're going to have to do that. That's enough questions for now."

He started to walk away, but she kept up with him. "Just a couple more, if you don't mind." She didn't give him a chance to answer. "Has anyone discovered Sullivan's motive in releasing the dogs a few months ago? Have you figured out what reason he could possibly have?"

Westley sighed. "Come on, Heidi, you've already asked me these questions. I didn't have answers then, and I still don't. I wish I did. Now, that's enough. I've got a case to work." He turned to the young man who'd clipped a leash on the collar. "All right, Rusty, get him to the vet and have him checked out, will you? The rest of you fan out and let's see if anyone's going to admit to missing a dog named Poco. Someone put that collar on him, and I want to know who it was. Don't let on that he's a base dog. Just act like he's a stray."

Rusty left with Patriot, while several members of the investigative team who'd been called in left to begin knocking on doors.

Westley nodded to Nick and Annie. "Are you still on Heidi duty?"

"I am."

Heidi duty? She grimaced, but let it go. Already, she was forming the article in her head while she continued to watch everything play out.

She finally nudged Nick. "Come on, let's go. I want to get the reaction of the neighbors being questioned at one in the morning."

He frowned. "I don't like that we're out in the open like this."

"I don't like it, either, but honestly, I'm not going to

let this guy keep me from doing my job. I've got a story to write and I need something to put in it." She scanned the area and, across the street, spotted two MPs on the front porch of the closest house. She headed that way and heard Nick's exasperated sigh. "Fine, I'll go and watch your back."

"Thanks." Although, she knew he might not spot a sniper. That worried her, but what was she going to do? Put her life on hold until whoever was after her was caught?

She grimaced. It might be the smart thing to do, but…" My dad wouldn't let this stop him," she said softly. "He'd go right into the fray and get the story."

"But—"

She cut off his words and shot him a sad smile. "I know. But he ended up dead. That's what you're thinking, aren't you?"

He shrugged. "Thinking, yes. Saying, no." He absently scratched Annie's ears and the dog leaned into him.

"It's okay. I can say it." She sighed and shook her head. "I just can't sit back and do nothing."

"I know. Let's just be careful."

"You're still sticking with me?"

"Those are the orders."

"Right." She looked at the ground. "Of course."

He tilted her chin to look her in the eye. "And if they weren't orders, I'd request them."

"You would?"

"I would."

"Why?"

"Because."

With another roll of her eyes, she did her best to hold

back the smile that wanted to spread across her face. "All right, then. Let's go."

They approached the nearest MP speaking to the sleepy-looking woman who'd opened the screen door. She shook her head. "I don't know anyone who owns a dog named Poco. Sorry. Can't believe you woke me up for that." She slammed the door.

Heidi shook her head.

They walked to the next home and for the next hour they got the same response—and several more slammed doors.

Nick cupped her elbow and brought her to a stop. "Are you ready to head back yet?"

With a sigh, she nodded. "I guess so. This is looking pretty pointless."

Nick turned her back toward his house. "What would you think of leaving the base? Going into hiding until all of this is resolved?"

"What do you think I think about that?"

"Right. I kind of figured that would be what you thought."

She bit her lip. "I can't hide, Nick. Even though that's my first instinct, I just can't do it. This guy wants me scared and cowering."

"No, I don't think he does."

"What do you mean?"

"I think he just wants you dead, Heidi, and that's what scares me."

TEN

"Come on, Heidi," Nick said. "There's nothing more to do here tonight."

She looked up from the little black notebook, then tucked it into her pocket with a sigh. "I guess you're right, but I've got some good stuff to work with."

"I suppose you're going to write this up for tomorrow," a voice said from behind Nick. He turned to see John Robinson looking at Heidi. That man was as annoying as a sandstorm.

"No, John, I'm going to ignore it—and my job. What do you think?"

The man's eyes flashed and he stepped closer to Heidi. "I think you'd better watch your step or I may have to go to Lou."

Nick ventured forward. "Hey, Robinson, you're out of line. Watch your space."

John looked back over his shoulder at Nick, then brushed past Heidi. She stumbled back a couple of steps and Nick reached forward to grasp her forearm. "You're dangerously close to assault, Robinson."

"Sorry, sorry." He held a hand up. "I stumbled." He smirked and stalked off.

Heidi stood glaring after the man and Nick turned

her toward his house. "Forget him for tonight. Let's go home."

"Yeah. I've got a story to write."

Nick's heart rate finally returned to normal after he shut the door on the outside world. And whoever wanted her dead. He'd been blunt with her a few minutes ago, but the truth was, he was scared for her. His immediate attraction to her the first time he'd met her months ago had sent him scurrying. There'd been no way he'd allow himself to be drawn to a reporter.

But now that he'd gotten to know her, all he wanted to do was protect her.

"You know you're not making this easy," he said, keeping his voice low so as not to wake his grandfather. Nick had sent the man a text just in case he woke up and wondered where they were. No return text said he'd probably slept through everything.

"Making what easy?"

"Keeping you safe."

"Oh." Her brows drew together. She went to sit on the couch and he followed her.

"Someone has shot at you and blown up your house, Heidi."

"I'm aware, thanks. But you know what I've noticed?"

"What's that?"

"Everything he's done has been so that he had a way to escape. The bombing of the training center? He had his escape plan in place. The shooting at the church? He was in a speeding car that got away. The bombing of my home? Same thing. He had it rigged to blow either at a certain time or when he could set off the explosion with a remote. A cell phone or something."

Nick frowned. She was right.

Heidi continued, "And he always seems to target me when there aren't many people around."

"So, you think if you're surrounded by people, you'll be all right?" he asked.

"It seems to look that way. Tonight, I was around a ton of people and he didn't try anything."

"I'm not sure that logic works."

She raked a hand through her hair. "I don't know. I just know that I can't hide." She stood and paced the room till she stopped by the mantel. "I'm taking precautions, I'm being careful. I'm not stupid and I don't have a death wish, but I won't hide."

He nodded. "I can't say I don't understand because I'd probably feel the same way if I were in your shoes."

"Really?"

"Yes. Didn't say I liked it, but I do understand."

"Thank you."

Standing, he held out a hand to her. She took it and stepped forward. "I'm headed for bed. You should do the same."

"I know. But I still have to write the story about Patriot's return. I'll see you in the morning?"

"I have an early meeting with Westley and Justin about the Red Rose Killer. What are your plans?"

"I have a meeting with Lou at eight thirty. Then I have to write up my latest personality piece." She smiled. "You wouldn't want to volunteer for a spot, would you?"

"Me? No, thanks."

"I figured, but I had to try."

"Go to bed, Heidi. We'll catch up tomorrow." Instead of letting her go, he pulled her close and slanted his lips across hers. It was an impromptu action that surprised him. And yet, he didn't regret it. The kiss lasted a few seconds before he ended it with a hug.

When he finally let go of her, she looked...bemused. "I hope that was okay."

"Oh, it was more than okay," she replied. "Confusing, but a good kiss."

He chuckled, then sighed. "I don't mean to be confusing. The more I'm around you, the more I like you. The more I like you, the more I question my sanity."

"Well... Thanks?"

Grimacing, he raked a hand through his short hair. "That didn't come out right. I'm conflicted about you, but not enough to stay away from you. How's that for honesty?"

Her eyes glittered up at him. "I like honesty. And I like you, too." She patted his cheek. "Good night, Nick."

And then she was walking away from him. He waited until he heard her door close before he went to bed. "Lord, don't let me mess this up. Protect Heidi from whoever is after her. And, Lord? Please, protect me from myself."

Morning came faster than Heidi would have liked and she found herself scrambling to beat the clock. Fatigue pulled at her as she got ready, and for the first time since taking the job at the base, she considered calling in sick. After everything that had happened, she didn't think Lou would give her any grief about it, but the thought of John Robinson had her pushing forward. Which was silly. Why did she even care what he thought?

She didn't, really. But she did care about her job and what her boss thought. Once she was dressed for the day, she reached for her recorder and the little black notebook and frowned when she couldn't find the recorder. She'd used both last night and had them in her jeans pocket. She'd only used her notebook last night to write the story about Patriot's return because she had everything she'd needed. She hadn't bothered to check the recording.

Where had she put it?

A glance at the clock sent her scurrying. No matter, she'd have to find it later. She stopped. But what if it was just lying around somewhere and someone picked it up? *No, please no.* She'd recorded her thoughts on just about everything she'd written in her little black notebook. If someone found it…

She scoured her room once more and when she came up empty, she gave a groan of frustration. She'd *really* have to find it later. But for now, being late wasn't an option. She slipped out the door and climbed into the rental her insurance company had delivered late last night.

Her own car had been parked in the driveway and had taken a hard hit when the house had exploded. Most likely, it would be declared a total loss. She tried not to be too depressed about the fact that her house, her car and all of her belongings were gone, but kept reminding herself that she had survived and no one else had been hurt. Doing her best to be grateful for that, she parked and made her way inside the newspaper office. She called out greetings to the few coworkers she passed as she headed to Lou's office.

He looked up at her knock. "Heidi! I didn't expect to see you this morning."

She frowned. "I emailed and told you I would be here."

"I got it, then saw John this morning and he said he wasn't sure you'd make it."

Anger seethed inside her. "John has no idea of my schedule. Please don't rely on his word."

Her boss gave her a shrewd look. "Everything okay between you two?"

Heidi gave him a tight smile. "Just fine, sir."

"Hmm." Heidi thought that sound held a world of skepticism but didn't bother to address it. She would handle John Robinson without dragging her boss into the fray. Only as a last resort would she bring her troubles to him.

"I'm here, sir," she said.

"Just wanted to say great job on the piece you sent last night. That was some mighty interesting stuff."

"Well, thanks, I appreciate that. I just happened to hear the commotion outside and joined in."

"I liked the dog story, too. We'll run that one tomorrow."

She frowned. "Wait a minute. Isn't the dog story what we were just talking about?"

He eyed her. "Are you losing it, Jenks?"

"I didn't think so until right now. Exactly what story are you talking about, sir?"

"I'm talking about the one you sent on how you overheard a conversation between two high-ranking investigative officials and their speculation that the serial killer is back on base. And how he was targeting everyone on the base now. I can't believe the guy actually called in and gave them a heads-up that he was going to start killing again and officials have covered it up." He leaned back and crossed his arms. "You're a sneaky one, aren't you?"

"Sneaky? Overheard?" She sputtered. "Wait a minute, I didn't write anything like that."

"I don't know where you got the information from,

but it's good. Just the kind of investigative reporting I like to see. Funny, I figured Robinson would explode when I told him I was printing it, but it didn't seem to faze him."

Panic rose within her. She leaned forward. "I didn't do a piece on the Red Rose Killer. Or the fact that he was back on base."

It was his turn to frown. "What are *you* talking about? You sent it about five hours ago. It went out in this morning's paper—and let me tell you, it was a chore to get it out on time. I know it's not a huge paper, but it's still a lot of work."

He picked up the paper sitting on the desk beside him and handed it to her. Heidi stared at the front-page headline—and her byline—in horror. SERIAL KILLER BACK ON BASE.

"I didn't send this! I didn't even write this. And it's not even true! No one said Sullivan called in with more threats. No one's covering anything up. Those are lies." She didn't have to read the article to know she didn't write it. "Lou, please tell me this isn't happening." She couldn't help reading a few lines, and her heart dipped into her shoes. "No, no, no, no, no. Oh, no. No one on this investigative team will talk to me ever again. I've got their trust now and this piece is going to kill it." Not to mention Nick. Oh, Nick…he would think… "How did you get this? From my email account?"

"Yep."

Heidi stood and paced in front of his desk. "I don't understand. How can this be?"

"Heidi, calm down. Are you telling me that you didn't send it?"

How many times did she have to say it? Placing her

palms on his desk, she leaned forward and looked him in the eye. "That's *exactly* what I'm telling you."

"Then you're telling me I just printed an article that can get me sued?"

She paused and bit her lip. "Yes. Maybe. The information is mostly accurate, but it wasn't supposed to be announced in the paper. I wasn't even supposed to know it. But the other parts are pure fiction." She slumped into the chair and covered her eyes. She was so done. No, she wasn't. She hadn't done this. How had this happened?

"How did this come from your email account, then?"

She narrowed her eyes. "John Robinson. He did this. Somehow, someway, he got that information and used it. He wants me off this paper and thinks he's found a way to make that happen. If no one will talk to me, what kind of reporter will I be?"

Lou scoffed. "What? Even if Robinson is inclined to do so, how would he get into your email?"

"I don't know, but he's resented me from day one. He was the only reporter on staff before the paper expanded to include me. All of a sudden, he had to share stories. I guess he doesn't like that." She picked up the paper again and settled back into the chair to read, ignoring the feel of his eyes boring into her.

The more she read, the sicker she came. "You have to do something," she finally whispered. "Print a retraction, something."

"But you said most of the information is accurate?"

"Yes, but some of it's not. It's going to cause panic on the base. The true elements are part of an ongoing investigation. As soon as Nick reads this, he's—" She bit her lip and fought the tears as she pictured his reaction. His feeling of betrayal.

"We'll fix the parts that are false, but the rest of the story stays."

"You realize this is just going to be fuel for the fire. Everyone is *really* going to think I'm the anonymous blogger now. They'll believe that not only am I releasing confidential information, I'm making stuff up. And I'm not! I only came by that information by accident and—"

Lou's tight jaw said he wasn't happy. At all. "All right, I'll talk to Robinson, but unless you have proof…"

"The proof is right there in front of you," she snapped. "I have to find Nick."

"Heidi—"

Her phone rang. She snagged it and lifted it to her ear. "Nick, I'm so sor—"

"This isn't Nick," the voice said. "This is Mark Hanson. You interviewed me about the stolen medals."

"Oh! I'm sorry, I thought you were someone else. How can I help you?" She was only half listening as her mind raced with how to explain this to Nick when she couldn't even explain it to herself. She'd jumped to the conclusion that John was behind the article, but could it be someone else? She couldn't imagine who.

"I've thought of something else you can add to the story," Hanson was saying. "I think I may know who the thief is."

He now had her attention. "Who?"

"No," he said, his voice now a whisper. "I think he's following me. I've got to go. Meet me in the alley behind the Winged Java in fifteen minutes and I'll tell you everything."

"No. Let's meet inside the cafe."

"I can't. He might see me! If you want the information, be there." He hung up.

She looked at her boss. "We're not done. I want a

meeting with you and John Robinson as soon as possible."

"I'll talk to him. Where are you going?"

"To find out who the medal thief is and then to find Nick to explain that I didn't write that article and have no idea how John got that information—" She stopped. Yes, she did know. When he'd bumped into her last night. He'd lifted her recorder from her jeans pocket and listened to it. And wrote that piece.

She spun on her heel and raced out the door.

Nick set the paper aside and pinched the bridge of his nose. Betrayal, hot and swift, flowed through him. He stood and threw his mug across his office. The ceramic shattered and spilled coffee to the floor.

Annie jumped to her feet and barked. He settled a hand on her head. "Sorry, girl. Didn't mean to scare you."

Justin appeared in the doorway. "Nick?"

"I can't believe she would do this." He tossed the paper onto his desk as though it might bite him.

"I saw the article this morning," Justin said. "Before the meeting."

"And you didn't say anything?"

"Wasn't sure what to say, to be honest. I know the blogger posted that we suspected Sullivan was back on base, but that was just conjecture on her part. That article, though, is about a direct conversation people will be more inclined to believe. But the other stuff...that's just not true. I figured you may have told her some of the facts she got right, and she made up the rest."

"I didn't tell her. She overheard Westley and me discussing it." Nick pressed his palms to his burning eyes and let out a humorless laugh. "She promised not to write it." His gaze met Justin's. "And I actually believed she wouldn't. And the stuff that's not true?" He shook his head. "I'm an idiot." He stood. "I'm supposed to be protecting her." That was going to be interesting. How he would manage to do that and keep his anger at her under control at the same time, he wasn't sure. It would be a huge test of his will.

"I put someone on her so you could be here for the meeting." Justin cleared his throat.

"I know. That's not what I meant. I'm supposed to be protecting her and right now, I don't even want to be around her." He glanced at the man leaning against the doorjamb. "I thought she was different."

"I did, too. I've never seen an article by her that wasn't well researched and well written. This one, though? It's like a different person wrote that piece."

"Well, it wasn't. Her name's right there under the headline."

"Yeah. Doesn't make sense."

"Oh, it makes sense all right." Bitterness, so potent he could taste it, rose within him. "I made a huge mistake trusting her. A reporter!" He slammed a hand on his desk and Annie woofed again. "Apparently, I'm as dim-witted as they come. I guess I just have to learn things the hard way."

"Ask her about it before you take her apart. She may have an explanation."

Nick reached for the phone. "Oh, you better believe I'm going to ask her. I'm going to find her right now." If anyone would know where she was, it would be her boss.

When Heidi pulled into the parking lot of the Winged Java, she noted it was busy and crowded. Probably why Mark wanted to meet her in the alleyway behind it.

She pulled around the side of the building, down the sidewalk and around back. Putting the car in Park, she looked around trying to spot the man. When she'd interviewed him two weeks ago, he'd been eager to tell his story and hadn't seemed like he was holding anything back. But if he'd decided he knew the thief, then she was going to find out.

She sat in her car for the next several minutes, watching, noting that it was a pretty deserted area. Which made her feel a little nervous. She hesitated. Was she doing the right thing? Her dad would have gone after the story. He would have met anyone, anytime, anywhere. But she wasn't her dad. She'd promised to be careful. This wasn't being careful.

She cranked the car and backed away from the alley. A shadow to her left made her jerk. Then her window shattered and glass rained down over her.

With a scream, Heidi hit the gas. The vehicle lurched forward and slammed into the side of the building.

A hard hand grabbed her ponytail. Pain shot through her head and down the base of her neck when her attacker yanked her from her car. She let out another scream and threw an elbow back. She connected and her attacker let out a harsh grunt.

His grip relaxed a fraction and Heidi lashed out with a foot, connecting with a hard knee. In a dark hoodie, the man cried out and went to the asphalt.

And she was free.

Until he lunged forward to wrap a hand around her ankle.

"Hey!"

The voice registered in her mind. Nick. Relief flowed through her, but she was still in the attacker's grip.

"Let her go!" Nick yelled.

The attacker's other hand reached inside his zippered hoodie, causing Heidi to scream. "He's going for a gun!"

In the next instant, somehow she was free.

The release of her ankle threw her off balance and she fell hard to her knees. Pain shot through her. She'd probably reopened the healing wounds, but at the moment that was the least of her worries.

Nick had his grip locked around her attacker's wrist and was wrestling him for the weapon.

ELEVEN

Nick's grip slipped and he clenched the muscles in his hand while he brought a knee up to the man's midsection. It was a glancing blow and did little damage other than to distract him a fraction. But it allowed Nick to get him on the ground.

In his peripheral vision, Nick saw a boot lash out. It connected with the side of the man's head and he went still, those icy blue eyes glazing over. The weapon fell from his hand and Nick scooped it up to aim it at him, then glanced up to see Isaac and Oliver. "Thanks. Can one of you check and see if he has any more weapons on him?"

A quick but thorough frisk by Oliver found him weapon-free. And glaring. Nick glanced at Heidi, noting her pale face, but set chin. "You okay?"

"Yes. Thanks."

He turned his attention back to the man on the ground. "Well, it's good to finally meet you," Nick said. Unfortunately, he didn't recognize him. Without taking his eyes from his captive, Nick asked, "The MPs on the way?"

"They are," Oliver said.

"Thanks for your help."

"Glad to do it," Isaac said. "What's the deal with this guy?"

Heidi stepped forward and looked at her attacker. "I recognize him. He's the one who blew up the training center—and probably my home."

"And shot at you in the parking lot of the church?" Nick asked.

"Possibly that, too."

The man on the ground moved as though to get up. "Stay put." Nick gestured with the gun.

The man stilled.

Two Security Forces vehicles pulled into the parking lot, lights flashing. The MPs approached, hands on their weapons. One covered the man and cuffed him while the other took the perp's weapon from Nick.

"What happened here?" that officer said.

"He attacked me," Heidi said, pointing to the blue-eyed man. She explained that he was the one she'd seen running from the training center just before it exploded.

"So, you're the one," one of the MPs said. "Let's go."

"Wait a minute," Nick said, stepping forward. "I'm part of the investigative team looking for Boyd Sullivan. We're not sure the bombing has anything to do with him, but do you mind if I ask this guy a couple of questions?"

"Go ahead."

Nick faced the cuffed assailant. "Why did you blow up the training center?"

"I didn't."

"Yes, you did," Heidi said.

"And if you don't cooperate, you're going away for attempted murder," Nick added.

The ice in those blue eyes melted a tad and a flicker of fear darkened them. "Murder! I didn't murder anyone."

"But you tried." At first, Nick didn't think the guy was going to talk. "Look, we've got you dead to rights here. We've got witnesses who saw your attack on Heidi. And she saw you come out of the training center just before it exploded. We've even got security footage of you." He snagged a handful of the hoodie and gave it a not-so-gentle yank before he dropped his hand. "This will match up to what's on video. You're going to go down for that. If you cooperate, you might get off with a lighter sentence. What's your name?"

The guy licked his lips and his shoulders dropped. "Airman Lance Gentry. And I really didn't mean for anyone to get hurt. The place was supposed to be empty."

"Right," Heidi said. "You didn't mean for anyone to get hurt. That's why you shot at me in the church parking lot."

He scowled. "Once I knew you could identify me…" He looked away. "I got scared," he said. "I had to get rid of you because I can't go anywhere on base without fear of being recognized. I can't live like that. If you were out of the picture, even if someone thought I was the guy, you wouldn't be around to confirm it." His eyes darted to the MPs listening to the exchange. "Guess I'm done now."

"Why are you doing all this?" Nick asked. "We know you went after Heidi because she could identify you. But why blow up the training center? That was the catalyst for all of this."

"Money. Why else?"

Nick exchanged a confused glance with Isaac and Oliver.

"Someone paid you to set the bomb?" Isaac asked.

"Yeah."

"Who?"

"I don't know his name, he didn't say. But he knew I needed money so he'd obviously done his homework on me."

"How did he contact you?"

"Knocked on the door at my house."

"Do you live on base?"

"Yeah." He looked down and scuffed his foot.

"But why stay here? Why take the risk of being caught? Especially since you knew Heidi could identify you if she saw you?"

Gentry lifted his head, nostrils flared. "He still owes me the other half of my money. I had to stay until he paid me. I've been looking for him, but haven't come across him yet. But he'll be back. I was just waiting for him to put in an appearance, then I was going to grab my money and get out of here."

"You could have lain low."

"Can't find a guy when you're not looking for him. I had to be out and about on the base. But every time I set foot outside my house, I was afraid someone was going to spot me."

Nick pulled his phone from the clip on his belt and tapped the screen. He pulled up the picture he kept on hand and showed it to the prisoner. "Is that the guy who came knocking?"

Gentry's brows knit and he frowned as he studied the picture. "That's Boyd Sullivan."

"No kidding."

"No, that's not him." Nick sighed and lowered the phone. "Wait. Let me see that again." Nick obliged. "You know, it's possible that could be him. The eyes look the same, but his hair was red and he had a beard."

"That doesn't surprise me. The man is a master of disguises."

"Whoa. Seriously?"

"Seriously," Nick said. "What else can you tell us? Did he say why he wanted the training center blown up?"

"When I asked, he just said he needed a distraction. He needed attention focused on something other than him."

Isaac gave a light snort. "Is he really that stupid to think that we would turn our attention to the explosion and off of him?"

Nick shrugged. "Well, it was one more thing to deal with. And it used resources and cost money. Sullivan is angry. He's out for revenge on those he feels have wronged him in some way. If he can cause us grief or inconvenience us in any way, he's going to do it."

Oliver nodded. "You've got a good read on him."

"I do."

"We done here?" The MPs were ready to get their prisoner to booking.

"We're done for now," Nick said. He turned to Heidi. "Done with him, anyway."

Heidi swallowed at the pure ice in Nick's eyes. She'd thought Gentry had a cold stare. He had nothing on Nick. "Can we talk?"

"We can," he answered in a clipped tone.

"Where?"

"Where we won't be overheard."

"Are you going to yell?" she asked him.

"Probably."

"Then let's go back to your place."

He eyed her with a flicker of confusion before his

gaze hardened once more into unreadable chips of blue. "Fine. My grandfather is out today volunteering at the food bank."

She started for the rental, then stopped. "I guess they'll need my car for evidence."

"They will. You can ride with me."

Not sure she wanted to, she nevertheless didn't argue and climbed in. The ride to his home was made in silence. Heidi almost broke it but decided against it.

When he still didn't speak as he led the way inside, Heidi got an inkling of just how livid he really was. Once in the den, he didn't sit. He simply crossed his arms and faced her, his jaw like granite.

"How did you know I was in trouble?"

"I didn't. I called your boss and asked him to tell me where you were."

"I'm sure glad of that." His glare hadn't lessened with the small talk. "I didn't write that article," she said.

He scoffed and shook his head. "And now you're going to lie to my face?"

Heidi bit her lip and sighed. "I have a feeling who did, but it wasn't me."

His frown deepened to the point she wondered if he'd ever be able to smile again. "How is that even possible? It's in the paper. With your byline."

"John Robinson is how it's possible," she spat. Just saying his name made her want to gag.

"Really? You're going to blame this on him? Your editor published it!"

"Because he thought it was from me! He didn't know I didn't write it."

Nick paced in front of the mantel and raked a hand over his head.

Heidi sighed. "I'm sorry, Nick. I—"

"How?"

"How what?"

"How did he get that information? That was a conversation between you and me and I asked you to keep it quiet. I didn't share that with anyone else who could have passed it on to Robinson."

"My recorder is missing. I think when John bumped into me last night after Patriot was found, he lifted the recorder from my pocket. I haven't had a chance to confront him, but I'm going to do that right now." She headed toward the door and stopped. "But I don't have a car."

"That's okay. I'm not planning to let you face him alone. You almost decked him one time. I think this time I need to come along to keep you from killing him."

Nostrils flaring, she gave him a tight nod. "I think that might be a good idea."

TWELVE

Nick didn't think he'd ever seen her so mad. Actually, the last person he'd seen this angry had been his grandfather when the story about his mother ran. When a person was this angry, it was hard to think straight.

That was why he was going along.

To make sure she didn't do anything that would get her court-martialed.

It didn't take long to track down Robinson. He was at his desk at the newspaper office. When he looked up and saw Heidi bearing down on him, Nick thought he saw a flash of fear in the man's eyes before he lifted his chin in defiance.

Heidi stopped at his desk. "I'd like to speak with you, if that's all right."

Admiring her calmness, Nick decided to stay back and let her handle it. At least until she decided to do him bodily harm.

John cleared his throat and rose. He grabbed his jacket and slipped into it. "Actually, I was just on my way out the door. I just got word that someone was arrested for the training center bombing—and that it's somehow related to the Red Rose Killer."

"Right. I was there."

Robinson froze. "What do you mean you were there? How were *you* there? How many times do I have to tell you that this is *my* story?"

"Then why do you have to steal my notes to get a story printed? Why are you trying so hard to discredit me?"

He flinched. "I don't have to stand here and listen to this garbage." He reached for his car keys and Heidi moved fast, swiping them from the desk. They hit the floor and skidded under the chair. "Hey!"

"You're not going anywhere until you tell Lou what you did." She crossed her arms.

"Are you nuts? You can't just come in here and act like this."

"Like what, John? Like a woman who is confronting a man who is not only a liar, but is willing to do just about anything to ruin her career?"

"I'm not—"

She stepped forward and Nick tensed. His phone rang and he shut it off, unwilling to have any distractions at the moment. He might have to intervene.

But Heidi didn't lift a hand, she simply thrust out her chin. "Yes, you are. You stole my recorder, listened to my notes and picked the one thing that would be sure to bring the hammer down on my head—and possibly my career. All you had to do was make sure those working the investigation wouldn't talk to me. How did you get into my email account?"

"Heidi, you're delusional. I don't know where you're getting all of this, but I've got to go."

"It should be easy enough to prove," Nick said.

Robinson stilled. "What are you talking about?"

"I'm talking about getting one of our IT people over here and letting them examine your computer. If you hacked into Heidi's account, it can be found. If you didn't, then no worries."

Robinson's face went bright red. "This is ridiculous! Get out of my space!"

"Have someone come over and check it out," a voice from behind Nick said.

Heidi spun. "Lou?"

Her boss shrugged and met Nick's gaze. "I don't want to think one of my reporters would do such a thing. Have someone come over and prove he didn't do it. That way, we'll shut everyone up."

"Lou." John rubbed his hand across his lips. "Really? You know I wouldn't—"

"Right. I do. But she doesn't. I'm doing this for her, too."

"Thanks, Lou," Heidi said.

"Don't thank me. You're going to feel pretty foolish when we prove you wrong."

She huffed. "I'll take that chance."

John's jaw got tighter. "Fine!" he exploded. "I did it."

Heidi blinked, her shock holding her silent for a moment. Had John actually admitted it? Nick nudged her and she snapped her mouth shut. Her shoulders slumped. "Why?" she whispered.

John groaned and dropped back into his chair. "Because I'm afraid I'm doing a lousy job on this story and just last week, I overheard Lou saying what a great reporter you were and I thought if I offered some kind of proof that you could possibly be the anonymous blogger— and were reporting false information on top of that—then Lou would get rid of you."

"So you were jealous?" She gaped, then shot a look

at her boss, who looked ready to stroke out at any moment. Her gaze swung back to Robinson.

He shrugged.

Heidi turned again to Lou, who gave a disgusted grunt and shook his head. "I'm disappointed in you, Robinson."

"I know, sir. I'm disappointed in myself."

"I should fire you."

Robinson flinched. "Sir..." He lifted a hand as though to argue his case. Then he dropped it. "Whatever you decide, sir."

"Don't fire him," Heidi said.

All eyes turned to her. "What?" Lou asked.

"You don't have to fire him."

"I can't let him get away with this."

"I agree. But...can you just take appropriate disciplinary action and let that be it?"

Lou stared at her for a few seconds before shaking his head. And Nick watched her, his expression a cross between pride and disbelief—and what she thought might be a smidge of admiration mixed in.

She shrugged. "Don't ask me to explain. I can't. I just know I don't want him fired."

"I'll print a retraction, then—or something," Lou said. "Actually, Robinson will. He'll print a confession."

"No," Nick said. "We don't want the paper's reputation to suffer."

"Then how are we going to fix this?" The man looked ready to explode.

"I think," Nick said, "you could have Heidi write a piece about how her email was compromised by someone she trusted, someone who's had a grudge against her and wanted to smear her name and the readers will buy it. Not only is it true, but with everything that's been happening to her—and the fact that she's been reporting on it—the readers will also be sympathetic that she's being targeted. Of course, she will talk about grateful she is for her boss's support and the support of the paper overall."

"I like that," Lou said.

"She can also point out how the paper holds to the highest standards of professionalism."

"Because that's true, too," Lou grunted. He turned his glare on John. "Get out of here until I can calm down long enough to think straight. I'll call you later and let you know what I've decided."

"Yes, sir." He shot a look at Heidi. "I'm sorry. That was lower than low and completely unprofessional. I'm sorry and, if I get to stay, it won't happen again, I promise."

Heidi nodded. As John left, she let out a low, slow breath and ran a hand over her hair. "Wow. I did *not* expect that."

"I don't think any of us did," Lou said.

She looked at Nick. "Can someone really tell if he hacked my email?"

"Probably. Truthfully, I have no idea. Are you ready to go or do you have something else you need to do here?"

She raised a brow at Lou and he waved a hand at her. "Go find a story." He headed for his office. "Preferably who the thief on this base is," he shot over his shoulder. "And I'm not talking about a recorder and story thief, I mean the guy stealing the medals!" His door slammed and Heidi flinched.

Then she cleared her throat. "What now?" she asked Nick.

"I think we should go back to my place and you should rest."

"Or write up my article you just assigned me."

He shot her a wry glance. "Sorry."

"No. It's brilliant. Thank you."

"Of course."

He took her hand and led her out of the building. She took a deep breath and looked around. "It's nice not to be looking over my shoulder and wondering if someone's going to try and kill me."

A low laugh escaped him. "I'm sure." Then he frowned. "But Sullivan is still on the loose. And if Gentry is to be believed, Sullivan had him blow up the center as a distraction, which means Sullivan still has plans. Evil plans, no doubt."

"So, what do we do?"

"We do what we can to find out who's stealing the medals." He looked away, then back at her. "Heidi, I—I apologize."

"To who? For what?"

"To you. For jumping down your throat about the article."

She shook her head. "You don't have to apologize for that. Your reaction was completely understandable."

"No. I knew better. Deep down, I really didn't think you'd do that, but when I couldn't find a better explanation…"

Heidi squeezed his hand. "Really, Nick. It's okay."

"Let me make it up to you."

"Hmm. Okay. How?"

"You feel like Mexican tonight?"

"That sounds good."

"So, I'll pick you up at six?"

She smiled. "How about we just meet at the front door?"

He laughed. "That works."

His phone rang, and he raised it to his ear. After a

moment a dark look spread across his face. "I understand," he said into the phone. "Thanks." He hung up.

Dread curled through her. "What is it?"

"Lance Gentry just escaped custody."

"What? How?"

"He attacked one of the MPs escorting him, got his weapon and took off on foot. They chased him and lost him in the woods. They're bringing the dogs out, but if he manages to get off base, he's as good as gone."

"He lives on base. He knows how to come and go without detection."

"Yeah. Which means we're back to looking over your shoulder."

THIRTEEN

Nick tugged at his collar and studied himself in the mirror. He couldn't believe how nervous he was. They'd decided to go ahead with dinner—and keep looking over their shoulders.

Gramps appeared in the bedroom doorway. "You look good, boy."

"Thanks."

"So why do you keep fidgeting with that collar?"

Nick dropped his hands. "Because I don't know what else to do with myself."

"She's come to mean a lot to you in a short time."

"She has. It scares me."

"Because she's a reporter?"

"Partly. I'm having second thoughts about this. I keep second-guessing myself. And her."

"It's your nature."

He huffed a short laugh. "I come by it honestly. When that story came out in the paper, I can't tell you how betrayed I felt. That feeling was not a good one and it never once occurred to me that she didn't write it."

"I can see why you're struggling, but you just have to talk through those times. But there has to be trust. If you can't trust her, you can't build a life with her."

"I know, Gramps."

"I know you do." He paused. "Your mother would like her."

A lump started to grow in the back of his throat and Nick cleared it away. He rubbed a hand over his eyes. "I think so, too. That's part of the struggle. I want to marry a girl Mom would approve of."

"I know, son. But truly, you can't go wrong with a girl who likes Mexican food."

Nick laughed, appreciating his grandfather's attempt to lighten the moment. "Maybe not."

His grandfather's expression sobered and his eyes narrowed. "She has a kind heart, Nick. Be gentle with it. But don't date her if you don't think you can work through the angst you still have about her."

Nick shook his head. "I think I'll talk to her, see what she's thinking. See if I learn anything new. I don't want to get hurt, but I don't want to hurt her, either. Maybe spending some time alone will help."

"Aw, you'll be all right. Now, let me get this for you." Gramps reached up and adjusted the collar, then patted Nick on the shoulder. "You look great, kid. She won't know what hit her."

Together, they walked out of the bedroom and into the foyer.

Heidi was pulling her coat off the rack. Nick stopped dead in his tracks when she turned and smiled. He gulped, wondering what happened to all the oxygen in the room.

His grandfather slapped him on the back. "I may have been wrong in my assessment."

"What do you mean?" he asked.

"I think it's you who doesn't know what hit him." He

hugged a startled Heidi. "Go easy on him, honey. He's out of practice with this dating stuff."

"Gramps!"

The old man laughed and strode into the den to turn the television on.

Nick blinked at her. "You look amazing."

"Thanks. So do you."

"So…uh…are you ready to go?"

"Whenever you are."

He helped her on with her coat and opened the door. Her light vanilla-scented fragrance followed her outside and he breathed deeply—only to stop when he came face-to-face with Justin Blackwood. Nick saluted, as did Heidi. "Sir?" Nick asked.

"Sorry to interrupt your evening, but we just got word that Bobby Stevens was attacked in the hospital."

Heidi gasped. "Oh, no! Is he all right?"

"He's wounded and under sedation right now, as well as heavy guard, but the doctor says he should be able to talk first thing in the morning. He's not to have visitors until then." He paused, his gaze on Heidi. "Because I want you there, I'm going to read you in on something that I need to stay out of the papers."

"Yes, sir."

"OSI Agent Steffen has been digging into Stevens's background, financial records, et cetera. At first, he couldn't find anything that set off any alarm bells."

"At first?" Heidi asked.

"As they kept digging, they expanded their search and found some interesting deposits into his mother's savings account. His name isn't on the account so it took some convincing to get a warrant for his mother's banking. Which is why it's taken this long to get back to you on Stevens."

"His mother has MS," Heidi said. "She's in a wheel-chair." She cleared her throat. "I guess that has nothing to do with what you're saying. Sorry."

"It has everything to do with it. He told you about her?"

"He did."

Justin nodded. "That's exactly what I'm talking about. You saved his life and you have a rapport with him. I'm guessing he's being paid to keep his mouth shut about something and I want to know what. Between the two of you, I want you to drag every scrap of information you can out of him. He knows something and it's time we knew it, too."

"Yes, sir," Heidi said. "I'm happy to talk to him. I'm glad he's going to be okay."

"Me, too."

"Captain?" Nick asked.

"Yes?"

"Why didn't you just call?"

"I did. You didn't answer your phone."

Nick sighed and pulled it from the clip. "Sorry, sir. I'd turned it off during a meeting. It's back on ring now. If you need anything else, I'll hear it."

Justin nodded, climbed into his vehicle and left.

"Poor Bobby," Heidi said. "I have a feeling he was up to no good at the training center the night it exploded, but he doesn't deserve this."

"I'm not sure I have quite as much sympathy." Nick took her hand. "Let's grab dinner and then get a good night's sleep. Tomorrow's going to be a long one."

By eight thirty in the morning, the hospital was a beehive of activity. And so was Heidi's brain. Determined to get some answers, she led the way to Bobby's room even while her mind relived the dinner from the night before. It had been nice—and weird. Nick had seemed a bit distant, as though he wanted to be there, but wasn't sure if he should be. She chalked it up to distraction due to the news about Bobby and the fact that Gentry had escaped. But they'd kept the conversation light, touching on a variety of topics before finally landing on the case of the stolen medals.

"Why do you think the thief's doing it?" Nick had asked. "They can't be worth that much."

"Some aren't, but there are a few that are. I think this guy doesn't know who has the ones worth money so he's having to break into every home and just grab the ones he can—along with any jewelry and cash he can find—and get out."

"I suppose."

"A lot of these families are multigenerational military. Some World War II medals are going for hundreds of thousands of dollars."

"That's crazy. It's not the piece of metal that should be worth anything, but the heroism behind them."

"I agree. Unfortunately, our thief doesn't."

"And he might be able to pass one or two off as worth more than they are. There's no telling."

"Right."

Now Heidi stood in front of the door that would lead her to the man who could possibly help them figure out who the thief was. And she wasn't leaving until he told them.

The security officer at the door stood and eyed them until Nick flashed his badge. He nodded and returned to his chair, his posture alert, eyes moving over each person in the hall. Heidi was glad to see him taking his responsibilities seriously.

"Hi there, may I help you?"

Heidi and Nick turned. A nurse in her early forties stood next to a cart with an open laptop.

"We're here to see Bobby Stevens," Nick said.

"I'm sorry, he's still pretty weak. I just came out of his room. The doctor upped his pain medication and he dropped back off to sleep. You might want to give him a few hours or come back after lunch."

Heidi frowned. "We were told he'd be able to talk this morning."

"Well, that person was wrong. Sorry."

Heidi sighed and exchanged a shrug with Nick. "All right, thanks. Guess we'll come back later. If I give you my number, will you let me know when he can talk?"

"Sure." Heidi gave it to her and the nurse moved to the next room.

Nick blew out a low breath. "Great."

"I have my laptop with me," Heidi said. "I guess I could head down to the cafeteria and get some work done on a couple of articles."

"We have a team meeting at eleven that I could make. Justin excused me from it so we could be here, but if we're not going to be able to talk to Stevens until after lunch, then I guess I'll head over there."

"All right. Go get caught up and come back and fill me in."

He quirked a smile. "A lot of it will be classified, sorry."

"I understand. I'll take whatever information you can give me and try to be happy with that. I'll let you know you when the nurse calls."

"Sounds good. I'll catch up with you later."

Nick arrived at the meeting ten minutes early. He slipped into the room and took a seat near the door, hoping Heidi would be safe while working in the hospital. If her attacker was smart, he'd be long gone by now, but the fact that Sullivan still owed him money meant he might still be hanging around. And that worried him. Only the fact that the hospital had security would allow him to focus his full attention on the forthcoming discussion.

Justin entered the conference room and set his briefcase on the table. "Nick, I'm surprised to see you here. Weren't you going to speak with Bobby Stevens?"

"Yes." Nick explained and Justin nodded.

"All right, you can head back over that way after the meeting."

Gretchen and Vanessa entered and took their seats at the table. Once everyone was accounted for, Justin opened by bringing everyone up to speed on the arrest and escape of Lance Gentry. "We managed to ask him some questions before he escaped. Not that I'm happy he's still out there, but I think he's given us everything he knows about Sullivan. There's no security footage at his home, so we're just going to have to believe that Sullivan showed up there. I believe it happened the way he described it." He looked at Vanessa. "Why don't you give us an update on Yvette Crenville?"

Vanessa shook her head. "We've been watching. Tag teaming it, so to speak. So far, there's nothing. She's gone to work, shopped for ridiculously priced health foods at the base market and spent any spare time doing yoga at the base gym. If she's an accomplice, we can't find any evidence of it."

Gretchen nodded her agreement.

"All right. I'm not ready to give up on her just yet. Keep up what you're doing and give us another report at the next meeting."

"Yes, sir." Gretchen nodded.

Vanessa also agreed.

"Let's move on to our next steps in finding Boyd Sullivan."

For the next two hours, they went over the case files, reviewing notes, interviews, and making more plans to track the man down.

Nick's phone rang just as they were wrapping things up and he motioned to Justin that he needed to take the call.

In the hall, he swiped the screen. "Hey, Heidi, everything okay?"

"That's sad."

"What?"

"The first question out of your mouth is asking if everything's okay."

He gave a low laugh. "Sorry, I guess it's become a habit at this point."

"I guess."

"What can I do for you?"

"The nurse just called me and said we should be able to talk to him in the next few minutes. I'm going to head to his room."

"Perfect, I'm headed that way."

Heidi tossed the remains of her snack into the trash and headed for the elevator. Once on the floor, she went straight to Bobby's room and showed her ID to the officer on duty.

"You might want to wait a minute before going in," the officer said. "The doctor's in there."

"What? The nurse just called and told me to come on up."

"Oh, well, he'll probably be done in a few minutes."

"I'll just stick my head in and let him know I'm here."

With a frown, she shoved open the door. To find a man in a white lab coat standing over Bobby Stevens, holding a pillow over his face.

She screamed and launched herself at the man, slamming into him. Heidi went to the floor while he stumbled back into the IV pole, cursed and landed beside her. Then he was on his feet. Heidi tried to get up, but at the last second, saw the hard fist swing at her. She rolled and his knuckles grazed her jaw. A flash of pain shot through her face and she lost her balance, falling to the floor once more. She landed on her backside with a grunt.

The door swung open and the officer ran in. "What's going—"

The attacker slammed a fist into the officer's face. His head snapped back and he crumpled to the floor. As the officer rolled, the man jerked the door open and bolted into the hall.

"Bobby?" Heidi gasped. Once again, she surged to her feet, ignoring the throbbing in her jaw. She hurried to Bobby's side. When she got a good look at him, she flinched at the sight of his new wounds. He had a puffy right cheek and a bruised eye. She went to him and grasped his hand. "Are you all right?"

Bobby nodded, breathing hard. "Yes. I'd just dozed off when I felt the pillow over my face. But yes, I'm okay."

Hospital personnel swarmed the room. A nurse was kneeling next to the fallen officer. She looked up. "We've alerted security."

Nick stepped inside. "Heidi? What's going on?"

It didn't take long to fill him in. He touched her

chin and she pulled back with a wince. "That's gotta hurt," he said.

"Yes, but, thankfully, it was just a glancing blow. I'll have a bruise, but nothing's broken."

"Did you see who it was?"

"No, not really. He was dressed like a doctor in a white coat but had on a baseball cap and sunglasses when he turned around. And before you ask, it could have been Lance Gentry, but I can't say for certain."

Once the officer was removed to receive more care and the doctor had checked out Bobby, he nodded to them. "You can have ten minutes. Then I want him resting again."

"Yes, sir," Nick said. The doctor left and Nick placed a hand on her shoulder. "Let me talk to him first, okay?"

"But the captain said…"

"I know what he said. Just go with me on this, will you? For now?"

She huffed and eyed him. He was up to something. "Fine. For now."

"Thanks." Nick opened the door and she followed him inside. Nick stepped up to the man's bed. "Bobby, who did this to you?"

"I—I don't know. It's all a little foggy."

"Maybe the attack is foggy, but I doubt the name of your attacker is," Nick said. "Who was it? Was it Lance Gentry?"

He flinched and then his expression shut down.

"Come on," Heidi said. "Without naming who it was, what happened with the previous attack? We know what happened this time." She rubbed a hand across her still-throbbing jaw.

"The previous attack?"

"Yes. When you got the bruises to your eye and cheek."

"I was asleep," Bobby said, his eyes locking on Heidi's. "When I woke up, I couldn't breathe. Someone was holding a pillow over my face—just like this time. I started flailing, trying to grab something, anything, to make him let go. My hand landed on my mug of ice and I managed to crack him in the head with it. He let go long enough for me to push the pillow off. Then he punched me. A nurse heard the commotion and ran in. The other guy bolted out and down the hall. This time was like an instant replay."

"Let me guess," Nick said. "He was wearing a hoodie."

"No, but a hat and sunglasses," Bobby muttered.

Leaning against the sink area, Nick hooked his thumbs into his pockets. "Why are you protecting someone who tried to kill you?" he asked.

Bobby huffed and crossed his arms. He looked away while his teeth worked his lower lip.

"Because he's scared," Heidi said softly. She stepped forward and took the young man's hand. He was probably just a few years younger than she, but she felt a lot older. Almost maternal in the way she wanted to not only help him, but smack him upside his head and demand he cooperate.

She controlled the second compulsion and squeezed his fingers. "Come on, Bobby. You're not helping yourself here. You're a victim of the bomber. Someone tried to kill you. Twice. Why won't you tell us what we need to know? What was Lance Gentry doing there?"

His fingers trembled in her grasp and a tear slid down his cheek. He quickly swiped it away and Heidi pretended she hadn't noticed. "It's…I…if I tell, he'll kill me."

"Looks like that's his goal anyway," Nick said. "Let me just share something with you. We know Lance Gentry set off the explosion in the training center. He's been trying to kill Heidi because he knows she can identify him. Guess what? He knows you can identify him, too. We had him in custody, but he escaped. So, if he's the one after you, he's still around to come back and finish the job. And it looks like he's pretty determined. What are you going to do when you get out of here? Run?"

"If I have to. Look, Lance Gentry isn't trying to kill me. He never knew that I saw him at the training center."

"Then why protect him?"

"It doesn't matter," Bobby said. "Don't you understand? I can't tell you anything."

Nick's nostrils flared. "Are you really that stupid?"

He all but shouted the question and Bobby sank into the pillows even while his eyes flashed a defiance that hadn't been there a few moments earlier.

Heidi rose. "Excuse us, Bobby, I need to have a word with First Lieutenant Donovan." She raised a brow at Nick. "Outside, please?"

"Heidi—"

She gripped his forearm and all but shoved him from the room. Once the door shut behind them, Nick frowned down at her. "What are you doing?"

"Trying to get the name of his attacker, but if you keep shouting at him, he's just going to close up tighter and tighter."

"I'm not shouting."

"You are. And you act like you've never questioned someone before. Can't you read his body language?"

He smiled. "Yes, ma'am."

"Ah." She gave him an assessing look. "I thought you were up to something. You planned this, didn't you?"

"And you played the good cop perfectly." He paced three steps down the hall, then back. "But I'm getting impatient. Go see if your more gentle approach works better. We know that Lance Gentry is the guy who attacked him. He knows we know. I want to know why he's protecting him."

"He seemed sincere when he said Lance never saw him."

"He's lying."

Heidi shook her head. "I don't think so. He has this tell when he lies. He rolls his eyes away from you, then looks down."

"Okay. Then if it wasn't Lance trying to kill him all this time, who is it?"

"I don't know."

"Then use those investigative skills and go find out." She grinned. "Stay tuned."

"I'm going to have hospital security come cover the door while I grab some coffee. You want one?"

"I'd love one," she said.

He stopped at the nurses' station to arrange the security and she reentered the room. Bobby had shut his eyes, but opened them when she sat next to him. "Look, Bobby, I know this isn't easy. I get it. I do. You say Lance Gentry isn't the one who attacked you, that he never knew you were there. Then where is all this coming from? You might as well tell us because we're not going to stop asking. What are you hiding? You were there at the training center before the explosion."

"Of course I was. I was taking care of the dogs."

"That's what you said before. But there weren't any

dogs in that part of the building, Bobby. Your story makes no sense."

He looked down and pleated the blanket with his fingers, then smoothed it out over his thighs.

Heidi sighed. "They found the money in your mother's bank account."

He froze. "What money?"

"Really?" She stared at him and his face crumbled. "What did someone pay you for? To keep quiet about the bombing?"

"No." His swift denial—and the fact that he met her gaze when he said it—had her believing him. Almost.

"Then what?" He sighed and rubbed his eyes. She pushed a little harder. "It's all going to come out in the long run," she said. "You might as well tell us what you know and catch a break legally."

"Do I need a lawyer?"

"Depends on what you were taking the money for."

Bobby hesitated only a moment before he said, "You were right. I was taking it to keep my mouth shut."

"About what?"

"About who was stealing the medals."

Finally. "I kind of thought so."

"I know who's stealing the medals, and he paid me to keep quiet."

"Then how does Lance Gentry fit into this and why would you protect him?"

"Because I saw him at the training center, and he saw me. He has a certain reputation and if he knew I blabbed about him, he'd come after me."

Heidi wanted to do a facepalm right there. "If you had told the MPs who he was, they could have caught him and you wouldn't have had to worry about him."

He laughed. "Right. Like he wouldn't have been released on bail or something." He shook his head. "I couldn't take the chance. But if you caught him and he escaped, then he's probably a long way away by now."

She was done with the Lance Gentry subject. "Who's the guy stealing the medals?"

"Roger Cooper. He's a senior airman. He's stealing the medals and hiding them in the kennel. The empty areas. I walked in early for my shift one afternoon because I needed an extra cage and we store some in that unused portion of the training center. He was there. When he saw me, he pulled a gun and said he'd pay me to keep my mouth shut. I agreed because I needed the money. Sometimes, he'd pass the medals off to me and I'd hide them for him when I went in to work."

"Where?"

"Different areas of the training center. Always away from the dogs, though, because you never know when someone's going to be around."

Heidi nodded. "Anything else you want to add?"

"No."

"So it was definitely Cooper who tried to kill you?"

"It was him. I saw him."

"Then you're going to press charges."

Fear flashed. "I don't know—"

"If you don't, he'll go free. And then he really will kill you. You do understand that, right?"

The man wilted against the pillow and gave a short nod followed by a wince. He lifted a hand to his head. "I understand. I just want all this to go away."

"Good. I'm sure OSI Special Agent Steffen will be by to take your statement." And conduct an arrest, but she kept that to herself. "You need to tell him everything you told me, okay? It needs to be officially on record."

"I get it. I will."

"Good." She stood and walked to the door. "I'm sorry it's ending this way for you, Bobby. I don't think you're a bad guy. I think you just got caught up in something a lot bigger than you. But you have the opportunity to turn this around and do the right thing. I suggest you take it."

A deep sigh filtered from him. "I know. I will. I actually feel better already now that it's off my chest."

When Nick returned with her coffee, she patted Bobby on the arm and they said their goodbyes. Two officers now stood guard outside the airman's room. She filled Nick in on the conversation with Bobby and he shook his head. "You're amazing."

"No, I just connected with Bobby when I saved his life. And he's really not a bad guy. I hope he can get his life straightened out at this point."

"His air force career is finished."

"I know. And so does he. He's just afraid. He's been afraid for a long time, but I think he feels better now that he's manned up and told the truth." She drew in a deep breath. "How's the officer who was hurt?" she asked. "Did you hear?"

"I checked on him. He has a fractured jaw, but he'll be all right."

"Wow, he really took a hard hit."

"He did."

She cleared her throat. "Okay, so what's next?"

"We look for this Roger Cooper character and see what we can shake loose from him."

"No, *I* look for Roger Cooper," Heidi said. "This is my story, Nick. Roger doesn't have anything to do with Boyd Sullivan."

His eyes narrowed. "Why don't we fill Justin in on

what we know and see what he says? Although, if you think about it, my orders are to protect you. So if you're going looking for Cooper, that means I am, too."

FOURTEEN

Nick returned to the car after searching for Cooper and slammed the door. "Another negative." Annie nudged the back of his head from her spot behind him and he reached back to scratch her ears.

"Great." Heidi sighed and rubbed her eyes. "And nothing from Justin?"

"Nope. They've got the MPs out in force looking for him and Gentry, but so far they don't have any solid leads as to where either could be."

"I get that Lance Gentry might be hard to find since he knows if he shows his face on base, he'll be caught, but how is it that no one has seen Roger Cooper lately? It's like he's dropped off the face of the planet."

They'd been tracking down Roger Cooper's known associates, asking information. Nick figured the easiest way to keep Heidi safe was to go along with the hunt. He had hopes that Justin and the Security Forces would find the man first, but it looked like none of them were going to find him.

Now they had only a couple of hours of daylight left. Nick really wanted them to locate the man before the sun went down, but he wasn't holding his breath.

"What did Captain Blackwood find after looking

into Cooper's background? Has he said when he'd have something?" she asked.

"Shortly."

"Okay, what now, then?"

"Let's grab something to eat. A drive-through." The longer he could keep her in the car, the easier it was to keep her out of danger. Between Gentry and Cooper, things could get deadly fast. He shuddered at the thought.

His phone buzzed. "Hold on. Justin just texted. He said Senior Airman Cooper has a spotless record. Which is why no one's thought twice about him being out with the flu the last four days."

"Does he live on base?"

Nick texted the question to Justin. "No. And the officers sent to his home said he wasn't there."

"Then he's hiding somewhere," Heidi said. "Close by if he's the one attacking Bobby at the hospital."

Nick nodded. "I'd be inclined to agree with that statement."

"Any local relatives?"

"No." He scrolled the text. "According to Justin, he has a sister in El Paso and a brother who's married with three kids, living in New Mexico."

"So he's not with them."

"Nope. Local authorities have already checked just as a way to cover their bases. He's here—somewhere. Justin's put a BOLO out on him." He stood. "I want to head to the kennels."

"Why? Aren't they already searching them?"

He shook his head. "I asked Justin if we could do it. With officers tied up searching for Gentry and Cooper, until I know for sure that Stevens is being straight with us, I'm not causing a scene or going on a wild-goose chase."

"Yeah. I see what you mean."

"So, let's go see what we can find."

With Annie in the back, Nick drove to the training center and parked close to the door.

He climbed out of the SUV and put on his backpack, then got Annie from her area and put her protective gear on. She sat and let him do what he needed to do with no protest. She knew she was going to work and her body quivered with excitement. Once they were ready, he scratched her ears, then looked at Heidi. "Stay behind us, okay? I don't know how safe this place is."

"Okay."

With Heidi behind him and Annie beside him, he pushed aside the yellow crime scene tape and led the way to the warped steel door. "I think the opening is big enough to get through. I don't know if you know the layout, but the door is higher than the ground floor. Once you're inside, you have to walk down three steps, okay?"

"I've been in there before. I know what you're talking about."

"Good. Let me go in first, then Annie, then I'll help you in if you need it."

Placing one foot carefully on the door, Nick had to climb over it and stop. The steps down had been destroyed and lay in crumbles two feet below. He hopped down. "Annie, come. Jump."

The dog scampered over the door and into his arms. He gave a grunt when she landed. "I think you've gained a few pounds, girl." She swiped a tongue across his face.

As always, her absolute trust in him never ceased to send a pang through his heart. Nick set the sixty-pound animal on the dirty, sooty floor and wiped the slobber from his cheek. He then turned back to warn Heidi.

"Watch it, the steps are gone."

"Got it."

With his hands holding her waist, he helped her through the opening. She placed her hand on his shoulders and he lowered her to the floor beside Annie.

"Thanks," she said.

"No problem." Even in the dim light of the broken building, she took his breath away. He didn't remove his hands from her waist immediately.

And she didn't step away from him.

"Heidi…"

"Yes?"

"I…uh…" What was he going to say? That he must be going crazy because he was crazy about *her*?

"Nick?"

"Yes, sorry." He dropped his hands and stepped back. He took his flashlight from his belt and clicked it on. The small windows lining the top edge of the wall just beneath the ceiling let in the waning natural light, but they needed the flashlight to illuminate the damage.

"Wow," she whispered as she looked around. "This is awful."

"No kidding."

"Why blow up this part of the kennel?" she asked. "I'm assuming Sullivan chose the location to bomb. Odd, I wouldn't think he'd care if he set off a bomb that killed people. It's almost like he picked an area that would cause damage, but wouldn't kill anyone. Human or animal."

"I don't think he cared whether he killed anyone or not. He probably picked this area because it's easy to get in and out of without being noticed and he could get the distraction he wanted."

"True."

They walked through the lobby and into the hall that would lead them to the large kennel area. "Where would you hide a bunch of medals if you were going to do so?" Nick asked.

"Someplace inconspicuous. Where no one would think to look—or accidentally stumble upon."

"That sounds about right. So, where is a nice inconspicuous place in a training center? The kennel?" He flashed the beam over the walls and then along the floor, looking for a path. There were large pieces of concrete and rubble that made the going slow down the hallway, but they kept at it until they reached the kennels. The outer door stood open. "It's not that bad back here. The bomb must have been set to go off near the entrance. It took the brunt of the blast. This is just soot from the smoke, and lots of standing water."

"Did they say what the bomb was made from?"

"C-4," he told her. "Annie found RDX, which is a common ingredient in the explosive."

"Where do you think he got it?"

"No telling. It's used with construction projects or demolition." He shrugged. "Could be from anywhere. And it's fairly stable. Like you have to set it off with a detonator."

"But you can attach a timer to that detonator, right?"

"Sure."

"Or use a remote to set it off?"

"Yes."

A noise behind them stopped him. "Did you hear that?" he asked her.

"I did. You think someone else is in here, too?"

"Shouldn't be," he said. "Unless one of the other investigators decided to come check it out, too."

"Or Roger Cooper's been hiding out here the whole time."

He nodded. "That was my next thought. Then again, it could just be the building shifting. It might not be safe. Hang back while I check it out, will you?"

"Not a chance."

"Heidi—"

"Nope."

He sighed. "Then at least stay behind me."

"I can do that."

Heidi did as he'd asked, but noted that Annie resisted the change in direction, pulling on her lead, wanting to go ahead.

"What is it, girl?" Nick muttered. "Go on. Show me what's got your attention."

A good handler always paid attention to his dog and Heidi realized that Nick wasn't just good, he was incredible, always completely in tune with Annie when they were working. The animal darted ahead to the end of the leash, sniffed around a pile of crates and then sat. Nick froze.

"What is it?" Heidi asked.

"Head for the entrance where we came in."

"Nick—"

"Just go! Now! Get out of here!"

One of the crates flew off and a figure rose from beneath it. "Don't move," he said.

Heidi stepped back and her heel caught against a piece of broken concrete. She fell back, landing hard on the debris, her phone skittering behind her. Her back protested the sudden stop and her palms scraped the floor, stinging. Gasping, she stared up at the man who held a weapon in one hand and something else in the other. A cardboard box sat beside his feet.

"Roger Cooper, I presume?" she asked, blindly reaching for her phone. She couldn't find it.

Nick stepped in front of her, hands raised in the surrender position. "Put it down, Cooper. It's all over for you."

"It's not over yet. At least not for me. But looks like you two showed up at the wrong time."

"Or the exact right time," Heidi said, ignoring the fear thrumming through her. Her fingers searched blindly for the phone, but she couldn't land on it. "We've been looking for you."

"I know. Everyone's looking for me."

"So you decided to hide out here?" Nick asked.

"Not exactly hiding."

"You're getting the medals so you can run, aren't you?" Heidi asked.

"Smart girl." His eyes flicked to Nick and Annie, then back to Heidi. "Only now, I've got to come up with a plan to get rid of you two."

"What are you doing with the bombs?"

"Insurance. Looks like that's going to pay off."

"So you're going to blow us up?" Heidi asked, hating the quiver in her voice.

"Not if you cooperate."

Nick shifted more fully in front of her. "What do you want us to do?"

"Walk. That way." Roger Cooper pointed with the hand he had clamped around the firing button, thumb hovering, ready to press it. Nick shuddered, his mind spinning for a way to get it away from the man. Tackling him might cause him to press the button.

Heidi moved, her foot catching on the rubble, and she stumbled against Nick. He caught her and pushed her behind him. Her hands landed on the small of his back, just under the Kevlar vest.

Her touch stirred his protective instincts in a way he didn't think he'd be able to explain if he had to. But one thing was for sure. Cooper was going to have to go through him to get to Heidi.

Nick eyed the man. "Is that the button that'll set that explosive off back there?"

"Yes, so don't try anything funny."

"Wouldn't think of it. What is it? C-4?"

"Like you don't know."

"So, what's the plan now?"

"I'm going to blow the place up. Some of those medals are worth a fortune, but it's obvious things are heating up and the investigation is getting too close. It's time for me to make my exit." He waved the firing button device. "Thanks to the guy who blew this place up the first time, I can now blow it again and everyone will think the original bomber did it."

"No, they won't," Heidi said.

Cooper frowned. "Why not?"

"Because the other bomber used a timer, not a firing button."

"It doesn't matter. It'll confuse the issue for a while and I'll be long gone."

Heidi's fingers trembled against his back and Nick couldn't help wondering where his backup was. He'd give anything to use his radio. Thankfully, Cooper hadn't told him to lose it yet.

"All right. New plan." Cooper licked his lips and his eyes darted over the training center. They hardened when they landed back on Nick. "Go to the kennels."

"What?"

"To the cages! Now!"

Annie gave a low growl and took a step forward. The man lowered the weapon to the dog and Nick placed a hand on her head. Annie calmed, but her fur still bristled. Nick took a step back and grasped Heidi's upper arm. "Go on," he said.

Heidi moved toward the kennels, making her way through the rubble once more. Nick stayed behind her, between her and the gunman. Would Cooper really do as he threatened? Maybe. He didn't seem to have any hesitation when it came to trying to kill Stevens. He didn't think the man wanted to die, but the uncertainty kept Nick from jumping him.

Once in the room with the kennel cages lining the walls, Cooper motioned to Nick. "Throw me your radio."

When Nick hesitated, he lifted the weapon and aimed it at Heidi. Nick tossed him the radio. Cooper gave it a hard kick and it skittered across the floor and out of the room. "Now your phone."

Nick complied.

Roger waved his hand with the firing button. "Get in."

The doors hung open, the locks swinging from the hooks.

"What's the plan once you lock us in the cage?" Nick

asked, stopping just short of entering the chain-link kennel.

"I get out of here."

"And blow us up," Heidi whispered.

The sound of sirens caught Nick's attention. And it caught Roger Cooper's as well. He paused and flicked a glance over his shoulder. That was the distraction Nick needed. He struck, launching himself at the man's hand and knocking the firing button to the floor.

FIFTEEN

Heidi bolted for the device while Nick and Cooper wrestled for control of his weapon, but Cooper's foot caught the small box and swept it from her reach.

The men rolled into her path and Heidi jumped back to avoid being hit. Only she moved a fraction too late. A boot landed on her calf and knocked her feet out from under her. She went down hard for the second time.

"Give it up, Cooper," Nick ordered.

The man didn't stop his desperate quest to escape. Over her shoulder she could see his hand reach for the firing button and then he screamed. Heidi flinched and rolled to her side to see Annie's jaws clamped down on the man's leg. He thrashed and kicked with his other leg, but Annie held fast—and Cooper didn't give up his attempts to gain control of the device.

Heidi scrambled toward it just as his hand landed on it and Nick's fist smashed into Cooper's face. He screamed again, but managed to clamp his fingers around the device.

And his thumb came down on the red button.

The explosion rocked the area. Nick rolled, covering Heidi with his body while the ceiling tiles fell. When the building settled, smoke and dust filled the room.

Coughing, gagging, Heidi tried to drag in a breath. She shoved at the heavy weight pinning her to the floor. "Nick. Move," she gasped.

He groaned and rolled. Pain engulfed her left arm and blood flowed from the wound. She clamped a hand over it, wondering how bad it was. "Nick, are you okay?"

He'd taken the brunt of the falling tiles. His vest had protected him some, but one had caught the back of his head and a river of blood trickled from his scalp. He coughed. "Yeah." He winced and lifted a hand to the back of his head. When he saw the blood on his fingers, he grimaced, then wiped his hand on his pants. "What about you?"

"I think so. Other than you crushing my lungs, I think I'm mostly unhurt." She looked around for Cooper. "He's gone."

"Annie!" Nick hauled himself to his feet and stumbled to the animal, who lay on her side. She whined and Nick settled down beside her, running his hands over her. "I think she's all right. Stunned, like us, a few cuts and scrapes, but okay." Annie proved him right by lurching to her feet. She shook herself and Nick gave her one more check before he turned to Heidi. "I'm going after him."

"I think he went toward the exit."

"He'd have to." He helped her to her feet and his expression changed when he saw her arm and her hand covered in blood. "You said you weren't hurt."

"I said *mostly* unhurt." She looked at the wound. "Looks like I can use a stitch or two, but I'm not worried about that right now. Let's go. We have a thief to catch."

Without questioning her further, he looped Annie's

leash over his wrist and held his weapon in that hand. "Let's try this again. Stay behind me, all right?"

"I'm here."

She stayed with him as he led the way toward the exit. The bomb had been more in the back this time, not the front, so there was no added rubble to trap them.

Until another explosion rocked the training center.

Once again, Nick pulled her to the ground while the ceiling fell down around them, along with part of the flooring above.

"Nick! What's going on?"

"Unbelievable," he muttered into the side of her neck. "He set that one off to trap us. To give him time to get out."

"But I heard the sirens. Law enforcement's here. He can't get away." She pushed herself to her feet, coughing, wheezing. "It's hard to breathe in here."

"I know. Pull your shirt up over your mouth and nose. It might help filter some of the dust." She did so while he pulled a bandanna from his pocket. "Here, use this."

"No, you use it. My shirt's working fine."

He wrapped the piece of cloth around the lower part of his face, then checked on Annie. She was panting and probably could use some fresh air and water just like he and Heidi. He rummaged through his pack and pulled out two bottles of water. And Annie's bowl. He handed a bottle to Heidi, who drank half of it. When Annie had her fill of the second bottle, Nick finished it off and tossed it aside. Then he reached into his pack and pulled out a mask that he fit over Annie's muzzle. It would filter some of the dust for her. "All right, let's figure out how to get out—or at least let someone know we're in here." He scrambled over the added debris and made his way to the huge pile blocking their exit

"I don't have my phone," Heidi said. "I lost it when I fell. Do you think we could find your radio?"

He hated the fear in her voice. "I don't know. I think it was probably buried in the first blast. My phone, too."

"What are we going to do?" she whispered.

Nick gripped her fingers. "We're going to stay calm and get out of this, okay?"

She gave him a slow nod. "All right. Tell me what I need to do."

"Let's take care of your arm, and then we'll have to assess the situation." Using supplies from his first aid kit he carried in the pack, he bandaged her arm. "That should hold you for now."

"It's fine. Thank you."

Together, they approached the pile of debris and Nick ran his hands over the mixture of tile and cement. He grabbed a piece and pulled. It slid loose and he tossed it aside. "I think we can try to dig our way out."

"They know we're in here, right?"

"They know. They'll be looking for us."

"They might think we're dead."

"Possibly. But they'll bring in search-and-rescue dogs and they'll alert we're here."

She grabbed a rock and shifted it. Debris tumbled, kicking up more dust. Choking, she shoved the rock aside and lifted her shirt to breathe through it. "Is that true or are you just saying that to make me feel better?"

"It's true." Nick stopped what he was doing and tore her shirt to make a mask. He tied it around her nose and mouth and went back to working.

Then she stopped. "Wait a minute. We can get out

through the kennel. We can crawl out the little doggie door and into the dog run."

Nick shook his head. "It's a good idea, but won't work. They keep those doggie doors locked as a security measure and only open them when there are dogs in the cages."

Her shoulders slumped. "Oh." Then she shrugged. "Okay, then. Back to digging."

For the next several minutes, they moved more of the debris, working quickly. Nick's head pounded a fierce rhythm, but the fact that they seemed to be making a little progress helped him push through the pain. Until nausea sent him to his knees.

Heidi dropped beside him. "Nick?"

"I'm okay. I just have to rest a second."

She pulled the water bottle from her pocket and held it out to him. "Drink."

"I'm fine."

"Quit being stubborn and drink it."

He did and then handed it back to her with a grunt. "I only agreed because I have another bottle in my pack. That one's yours, okay?"

"We'll split it if we have to," she said.

"We'll see." He paused. "I owe you an apology."

"What? No, you don't."

"Actually I do. I want to apologize for getting you into this. I should have left you outside the building while I investigated."

She huffed a short laugh. "You really think you could have talked me into that?"

"I should have tried, anyway."

"Rest easy, Nick. You would have failed."

He laughed. "You're very stubborn."

"I know. How are you feeling?"

"Better, thanks." He rose and spotted a steel rod about five feet long. "Let's see if this does anything."

Nick started to insert the rod in between two rocks, then stopped to grab Heidi's arm. "You hear that?"

"No. What?"

The distinct sound of barking.

Annie's ears perked up and she rose from her spot on the floor. She gave a low woof through the mask and stepped over the debris. Nick worked the rod like a crowbar and managed to send more tile and concrete falling from the pile to the floor. Then he pressed it into the small opening and sent the same rolling down on the other side. A whoosh of stale air hit him in the face and relief flowed through him. "Hey! Back here!" he yelled.

The barking intensified and Annie answered with three short barks of her own.

"At least she'll lead them this way," Heidi said.

Nick continued to roll the remnants of the ceiling from the pile. Workers started in on the other side and soon, there was a hole large enough for Heidi to crawl through. He helped her scramble through it and then picked up Annie. "Got a dog coming through. Someone needs to catch her. She's got on her boots so she can walk."

"Hand her through," a voice called. He thought it might be Isaac Goddard. Ignoring his throbbing, swimming head, Nick passed Annie through the opening, then crawled up to shove his head and arms through.

Hands grasped his wrists and pulled.

And he was finally on the other side. Isaac greeted him with a slap on the back. Justin and Westley were checking Annie out. A paramedic was trying to get

Heidi to go with him. Only she shook her head. "Not until Nick's free."

"I'm here, Heidi."

She spun and ran over to throw herself in his arms. He grasped her tight. "We made it," she whispered.

"I know." He glanced at Justin, whose brows rose at the sight of Heidi in Nick's arms. Nick ignored the look and instead asked, "Did you happen to catch the guy responsible for this? Roger Cooper."

"He's outside," Justin replied. "Wrapped up nice and tight, with his rights read to him and everything."

"How did you know it was him?"

"He tried to run with a big ole box of medals. We figure he's the one who's been breaking into houses and stealing them along with whatever cash and jewelry he could find."

"You figure right."

"He set off the explosions, too," Heidi said.

"And we found more on him," Justin explained. "C-4 and firing buttons. The bomb squad is here and is going to search the building for more."

"Do you need Annie and me?" Nick asked.

"No." Justin clapped him on the shoulder. "You and Heidi are going to the hospital to get checked out, Annie's going to the vet, and then you've got a couple of days off to recuperate. Annie might the best bomb dog on base, but she's not the only one."

"I don't need a hospital, sir," Heidi said.

"Doesn't matter, you're getting one."

"Yes, sir."

Nick knew he'd get the same answer if he protested the hospital so he simply kept his mouth shut.

"Anyone find Lance Gentry yet?"

"Not yet," Justin said. "But we got a lead he stole a

car. We've got a BOLO out on it. I'll let you know as soon as he's in custody."

"Thanks. You'll have to leave a message. My phone and radio are buried in there somewhere."

"I'll have a phone delivered to the hospital. Until Gentry's caught, you don't need to be without one. Now, we need statements."

It didn't take long to finish up their statements. Annie headed for the base veterinarian and Nick and Heidi were transported to the hospital. A young airman met them there. "I was told to deliver this to you." He handed Nick a phone.

"Thanks."

"You're welcome."

He left and Nick watched Heidi as they rolled her into the adjoining examination room, suppressing the urge to race after her.

"All right, sir, let's get you transferred to the bed and take a look at that head."

His attention only slightly diverted by the nurse, Nick decided to do his best to cooperate and hurry this whole unnecessary checkup along so he could rejoin Heidi and—what?

What would he say when he saw her? While the nurse shaved a small patch at the back of his head for the two stitches deemed necessary, Nick silently planned the words he'd say to Heidi—if he could gather his nerve. When his phone rang, he grabbed it, grateful for the interruption. Ignoring the glare from the nurse, he answered it.

When the doctor removed the bandage Nick had applied at the kennels, Heidi got her first look at the wound on her arm and grimaced. It wasn't pretty. But once it was cleaned and re-bandaged, she was ready to go. "I have a couple of articles to write," she told the nurse. "I need to get going."

"You'll be out of here soon enough," she said and left the room.

Heidi leaned back with a groan and closed her eyes. She was exhausted, but couldn't shut her mind off. All she could think about was Nick—and ceilings caving in.

Being trapped with him had been scary enough. If he hadn't been there with her—

She shuddered.

The door opened. "That was fast," she said, not bothering to open her eyes since she assumed it was the nurse.

Tender fingers on her cheek brought her eyes open. Nick stood there, gazing at her with a look on his face that made her pulse pick up speed. "Nick?"

"I don't know how it happened," he said.

She swallowed. "What?"

"You got under my skin."

"Oh. I think you mentioned that once upon a time."

"In a good way."

"I like you, too, Nick."

He laughed and leaned over to kiss her. His lips on hers sent her pulse into overdrive. Warmth infused her and she realized she could get used to this on a daily basis. He pulled away with a pained groan and lifted a hand to his head.

She sat up. "Nick? You okay?"

"Yeah, I just can't kiss you bending over like that. Makes my head pound."

"Hmm. Makes my *heart* pound."

"Ha. Mine, too." He sighed and hugged her to him. "What am I going to do with you?"

"Oh, I don't know. Maybe take me out on a date?"

His laughter rumbled beneath her ear. "I think that can be arranged."

"Just not a shopping date. No shopping."

More laughter. "I like shopping with you."

"Hmm. Well, it wasn't too bad, I suppose. The fudge part was great."

"Wow. Thanks."

"Okay, how about this?" she said. "No bullets or bombs allowed on the date. Just fudge."

"Definitely. That's one rule I think we can follow now that Lance Gentry, Roger Cooper and Bobby Stevens are all under lock and key."

"They found Lance?"

"Justin called while I was getting looked at. They caught Gentry at the airport trying to board a plane. Someone recognized the car he'd stolen and called it in."

"Well, that was stupid of him."

"It was only a matter of time before he messed up."

She sighed. "Good. I'm glad he's no longer a threat to anyone. I still feel kind of sorry for Bobby, though. I think he just got mixed up with the wrong people and couldn't find a way out without disappointing his mother."

"I think you may be right, but unfortunately, there are consequences for our choices."

"True."

The door opened and the doctor entered. "Oh, hey, Nick."

"Porter Davenport, good to see you." The two men shook hands. "How's my girl here?"

My girl?

"Your girl?" the doctor asked. "I see a lot has happened in the two weeks since we last had lunch," he said as he turned toward Heidi.

She bit her lip, intrigued by Nick's sudden and interesting shade of red even as happiness suffused her. "Um, Heidi, this is Porter Davenport. He and I have been friends for a while now."

"Nice to meet you," she said. She liked being referred to as Nick's girl. A lot. And it looked like he wasn't going to be shy about letting others know he'd staked his claim. Wow. That was a lot to think about. And she would. Later. In the privacy of her room, where she could ponder what the future might hold.

Right now, she was ready to get out of here. She had articles to write. She could think about her feelings toward Nick later. Like whether or not she loved him. The thought made her mouth go dry and her throat constrict. Oh, boy. Love? Maybe.

"Let's find out."

She gasped. "Find out? Find out what?"

The doctor stepped over. "Find out how you are."

"Oh. Right. Thank you."

He checked her eyes, her breathing and her pulse one more time. When he straightened, he nodded. "Pulse is a little fast."

No doubt. Heidi's flush deepened and she met Nick's wicked gaze. "Well, it's been an interesting few hours," she murmured.

"I heard what happened at the training center," Porter said. "Another blast. Unbelievable."

"No kidding," Heidi said. "And technically, it was two more blasts, but who's counting at this point? Fortunately, everything took place in that area that's deserted. It'll have to be completely razed and rebuilt, but at least no one was hurt this time."

He smiled. "Well, it looks like you two were incredibly fortunate. A few bumps and bruises, but no lasting damage. I'd say you definitely had someone watching over you."

"God just wasn't ready to take us yet, I guess," Heidi said.

Porter raised a brow and nodded. "I guess not." He turned and shook hands with Nick again. "And I, for one, am very glad of that fact." He backed toward the door. "Nice to meet you, Heidi. Take care of that arm and get some rest."

"I will. Thank you."

He left, and the nurse returned with her discharge papers—and Nick's. By the time they walked out of the hospital, the sun was creeping up over the horizon.

Nick wrapped an arm around her shoulders. "Are you hungry?"

"Starved."

"Feel like going on that date now?"

She laughed. "What? Now? No way. I'm a mess. I need a shower and a nap."

"All right, how does pizza sound?"

"For breakfast?" She shrugged. "As long as it's delivered."

"Of course."

"Then that sounds amazing."

He pulled out his new phone and placed the order at the twenty-four-hour pizza place while they walked.

The cool morning air was refreshing and Heidi breathed in. "I'll never take being able to breathe clean air for granted again," she said when he hung up.

"I know what you mean."

It didn't take long to reach his home. "Is your grandfather here?"

"No, playing golf." He glanced at his watch. "His tee time is in fifteen minutes, I think. He texted me a little while ago."

"You didn't tell him what was going on?"

"No, just that we were working. I'm sure he heard about the explosions at the training center. Again. But he's used to my hours and doesn't get stressed about it when I'm gone."

"That's nice. And he's really gotten into the whole golf thing, hasn't he?"

He smiled. "It's good for him. The first few months after my grandmother died, he didn't really know what to do with himself, but he's adjusting—and learning to enjoy life again."

Once inside Nick's home, they both took the time to clean up and change before meeting back in the kitchen. Nick started to pull plates and glasses from the cupboard when the doorbell rang. "That was fast."

"Not fast enough." She darted for the door and Nick laughed. "Why don't you get that?"

She returned with the pizza box in one hand, a slice missing a bite in the other. Chewing, she set the box on the table. "Mmm...so good."

Nick laughed. And laughed again.

SIXTEEN

One week later

Heidi walked into Lou's office and took a seat in the chair opposite her boss. "What's up?"

Lou pursed his lips and set aside his reading glasses. "It's been a long few months with this serial killer on the loose."

"I know. The whole base is still on pins and needles." They both knew this, so where was this going?

"I've come to a decision, and Robinson isn't going to like it."

She frowned. "Okay." Since when did Lou run his decisions by her?

"You've really proven yourself over the last few weeks. Your personality pieces are really popular, you caught the person stealing medals from the homes, helped catch the person who bombed the training center and almost died for your efforts."

So, he'd noticed. "Well, I didn't catch the person all by myself. I had a little help there."

"Whatever. I think it's time you were rewarded for your efforts," he said.

"Rewarded?"

"Yep. I'm making you senior reporter. I may be gruff, but I'm honest and I want this paper to reflect integrity. If our readers don't trust us, they're not going to read us."

"True." She managed to get the word out, but "senior reporter" kept echoing in her mind.

"And Robinson messed up in a big way. Thankfully, because of your and Donovan's willingness not to bring to light Robinson's deception, the people are none the wiser. But I can't risk it happening again. I trust you, Heidi. Unfortunately, I don't trust Robinson. He's going to have to work his way back to that."

"Sir—" Heidi's mouth opened, then closed. What did she say? Stunned, she couldn't find any words.

"So, do you want the job or not?"

"Or course, but John's not going to be happy about this. Working with him may be...uncomfortable." To put it mildly.

"Robinson will do what I tell him or he'll be looking for another job. He should be on his face with gratitude that I didn't fire him."

"I agree with that."

"Good. Now get out of here and go find me that serial killer."

Nerves tingling, excitement growing by the second, Heidi stood and rubbed her palms down her uniform pants. "Yes, sir."

She paused and Lou looked up. "What is it?" he barked.

"Thank you, sir. I really appreciate this opportunity."

"I know you do. Now scram."

Heidi did so, her heart light. And the first person she wanted to tell was Nick. She texted him. Can you talk?

Sure. His immediate response made her smile.

A second later, her phone rang. "I got promoted," she blurted on answering, and told him everything.

"No way. Heidi, that's amazing!"

"I know!"

"Let's celebrate."

"Okay, when and where?"

Once they had it set up, Heidi checked her schedule. "I've got to run. I'm meeting Vanessa Gomez at the hospital. She's agreed to let me interview her."

"I'll be honest, I'm nervous about you being so close to this serial killer case. It was one thing when you were just on the base where Sullivan might be also, but you're not one of his targets. Being actively involved in reporting on Sullivan might change that. I have to admit, it scares me. A lot."

"I'm careful, Nick. You know me."

"Yeah, I do."

She laughed. "Don't sound so morose." Turning serious, she said, "I promise, Nick, I'll be careful. No stupid moves on my part that put me in danger. Trust me, I've got too much to live for."

She hung up and headed for the hospital. It didn't take her long to find the cafeteria where Vanessa had agreed to meet. Heidi saw the woman sitting in the back, in a corner where she could watch the comings and goings of everyone in the place.

Heidi slid into the seat opposite her. "Hi."

"Hi."

"Thanks for agreeing to talk to me."

"Sure. I'm so sick of Boyd Sullivan and everything he's getting away with. If talking to you will help catch him faster, then I'm all for it."

"Okay, then just start at the beginning. I'll record your story, if that's all right."

"It's fine." Once Heidi had everything set up, she nodded. Vanessa drew in a deep breath. "Back in April, I received a rose in my mailbox. Along with a note saying, *I'm coming for you.* I was shocked. I simply had no idea why Boyd would target me. I only saw him a couple of times on base, and one of those times, I actually helped him out. He was kind. I was nice and professional and did him a favor."

"What kind of favor?"

Vanessa ran a hand over her hair. "Boyd got into a fight with someone. He was pretty beat up and came to me because he needed some stitches. He didn't want to go through official channels because he knew he'd be reprimanded." She shrugged. "At first, I was going to say no, but I was drawn to him. I felt sorry for him."

"You had a romantic thing going on?"

Vanessa recoiled. "What? No! Don't print that!"

Heidi held up a hand. "No, I won't, I promise. It's just that's what it kind of sounded like."

"Well, that's not it. When I say I was drawn to him, I just meant that Boyd reminded me so much of my brother, Aiden, that I simply couldn't refuse. I mean, if Aiden ever found himself in a similar situation, I would hope there would be someone there for him, you know?"

Interesting. "I understand. So, what was it about him that reminded you of your brother?"

"I'm not really sure I can put my finger on it. Maybe an intense restlessness or a boiling anger with no outlet or release."

"That would make sense. The anger part at least."

Vanessa frowned. "I guess. But one can be very angry without becoming a serial killer."

"Yeah. Too bad Boyd Sullivan didn't get that memo."

"Indeed. Now—"

An announcement over the PA system stopped her. She listened, then stood. "I'm sorry, I have to go. That's an emergency. If you have more questions, feel free to call me later and we can try to get together again when I'm not working."

With that, she was gone. "I do have more questions." But they could wait.

A hint of familiar cologne tingled her nose seconds before the kiss on the side of her neck made her smile. And forget all about stories and serial killers and busy nurses.

"Hey, you," Nick said. "Can I sweep you off your feet and take you to lunch?"

She turned to kiss him, a slow, leisurely melding of their lips that she wanted to go on forever. Except they had an audience. She pulled back, but couldn't resist one last quick peck. "You've already swept me off my feet, but you can certainly do it again."

"Come on out by the fountain. Annie and I have something we need to ask you."

"You can't ask me here?"

"Nope."

"All right, then."

He led her out a side door to the beautiful fountain surrounded by a three-foot brick wall. The fountain was set in the middle of a small grassy area that had a peaceful parklike feel to it. Annie settled into a shady spot and put her head between her paws. But she never took her eyes off Nick.

Heidi spotted a bouquet of flowers sitting on the wall and gasped. "Nick? Pink carnations?"

"Yes." He picked them up and pressed them into her arms.

She sniffed them and smiled. "Thank you. This is so sweet."

"That's not all."

"What else is there?"

"That thing I wanted to ask you."

"Ah…right. Okay."

"Heidi, you make me laugh. I can't believe how much you make me laugh." He cleared his throat. "I like that about you, Heidi."

"Well, thank you. I like a lot about you, too. In fact…" She paused. Did she dare say it? She drew in a deep breath. "I may even love some things about you."

He kissed her. Then drew back. "Stop doing that."

She blinked. "What?"

"Distracting me or I'll never get this said."

"Oh. Sorry."

He cleared his throat again. "Annie keeps looking at me."

"What does that have to do with anything?"

"A lot." He dropped to his knees in front of her and her heart stopped. Then pounded hard enough to echo in her ears.

"Nick?" she whispered.

"I have a confession to make—I'm an idiot."

"It happens to the best of us sometimes." She paused while he laughed. "I'm teasing," she said. "What are you talking about? You're not an idiot."

"I've been trying to think of the words for days now, but I can't find the exact right ones."

"For what?"

"You deserve better. A better place to be proposed to, a better, more romantic guy with the right words, a slow, drawn-out proposal with all the bells and whistles, but the truth is, Heidi, I'm impatient—one of my many flaws you'll learn about, I'm afraid—and I need to say this before I explode. I'm in love with you and I want to marry you. Am I crazy in hoping you feel the same way?"

Tears had started dripping down her cheeks by the time he reached the words, "I'm in love with you and I want to marry you." She sniffed. "You're not crazy," she whispered. "Not about this, anyway. This is a beautiful place. And I don't need bells and whistles, I just need you."

"Oh, good." His shoulders lost their military rigidness for a brief moment. "That's a relief." He dug into his pocket and pulled out a ring.

Heidi let out a gasp. "Nick?"

"It was my mother's," he said. "And her mother's before that. I'd be honored if you'd wear it. But if you don't like it or it's not your style, we'll go find something else."

She swallowed and took the ring from him. "It's gorgeous." The white gold setting held a teardrop diamond that was dainty and feminine. She loved it. Because of the history behind it but mostly because of the man who gave it to her. "I'd be proud and honored to wear it."

"Really?"

"Yes, Nick, really."

He kissed her, long and hard. Then set her away from him, but let his fingers trail down her cheek before he dropped his hand. "Want to go eat lunch and celebrate?"

She couldn't stop the grin. "I do."

"Just the words I can't wait to hear again in a church setting."

They rushed out to Nick's vehicle and Heidi climbed in and Nick let Annie into her area. Heidi glanced at her in the rearview mirror.

And thought the dog was smiling.

* * * * *

The hunt for the Red Rose Killer continues.
Look for the next exciting stories in the
MILITARY K-9 UNIT *series.*

Dear Reader,

Thank you so much for coming along on Nick and Heidi's exciting adventure. Both characters had a lot to learn in this story and I think they were wise enough to take advantage of the opportunities to grow. Heidi had to curb her impatience when it came to working with a coworker who drove her crazy. In addition to that, she had to decide to be ethical and do her best on a story she wasn't super interested in doing. I was proud of her for doing that. ☺ I do hope you'll be sure to get the other books in the series. Don't forget, there are EIGHT books in this series, so make sure you have them all. Thank you again for reading. Be sure to check out my facebook page and join in the fun there. www.facebook.com/lynetteeason and my website, www.lynetteeason.com.

God Bless,
Lynette Eason

Get 4 FREE REWARDS!

We'll send you 2 FREE Books plus <u>2 FREE</u> Mystery Gifts.

Love Inspired® Suspense books feature Christian characters facing challenges to their faith... and lives.

FREE Value Over $20

YES! Please send me 2 FREE Love Inspired® Suspense novels and my 2 FREE mystery gifts (gifts are worth about $10 retail). After receiving them, if I don't wish to receive any more books, I can return the shipping statement marked "cancel." If I don't cancel, I will receive 4 brand-new novels every month and be billed just $5.24 each for the regular-print edition or $5.74 each for the larger-print edition in the U.S., or $5.74 each for the regular-print edition or $6.24 each for the larger-print edition in Canada. That's a savings of at least 13% off the cover price. It's quite a bargain! Shipping and handling is just 50¢ per book in the U.S. and 75¢ per book in Canada*. I understand that accepting the 2 free books and gifts places me under no obligation to buy anything. I can always return a shipment and cancel at any time. The free books and gifts are mine to keep no matter what I decide.

Choose one: ☐ **Love Inspired® Suspense** ☐ **Love Inspired® Suspense**
                     Regular-Print   Larger-Print
                     (153/353 IDN GMY5)   (107/307 IDN GMY5)

Name (please print)

Address   Apt. #

City   State/Province   Zip/Postal Code

Mail to the **Reader Service:**
IN U.S.A.: P.O. Box 1341, Buffalo, NY 14240-8531
IN CANADA: P.O. Box 603, Fort Erie, Ontario L2A 5X3

Want to try two free books from another series! Call 1-800-873-8635 or visit www.ReaderService.com.

---

*Terms and prices subject to change without notice. Prices do not include applicable taxes. Sales tax applicable in N.Y. Canadian residents will be charged applicable taxes. Offer not valid in Quebec. This offer is limited to one order per household. Books received may not be as shown. Not valid for current subscribers to Love Inspired Suspense books. All orders subject to approval. Credit or debit balances in a customer's account(s) may be offset by any other outstanding balance owed by or to the customer. Please allow 4 to 6 weeks for delivery. Offer available while quantities last.

Your Privacy—The Reader Service is committed to protecting your privacy. Our Privacy Policy is available online at www.ReaderService.com or upon request from the Reader Service. We make a portion of our mailing list available to reputable third parties that offer products we believe may interest you. If you prefer that we not exchange your name with third parties, or if you wish to clarify or modify your communication preferences, please visit us at www.ReaderService.com/consumerschoice or write to us at Reader Service Preference Service, P.O. Box 9062, Buffalo, NY 14240-9062. Include your complete name and address.

LIS18

Two fatal drug overdoses in the past week.

Exhausted from her thirteen-hour shift in the critical care unit, First Lieutenant Vanessa Gomez made her way down the hallway of the Canyon Air Force Base hospital, grappling with the impact of this latest drug-related death.

The corridor lights abruptly went out, enclosing her in complete darkness. She froze, instinctively searching for the nearest exit sign, when strong hands roughly grabbed her from behind, long fingers wrapping themselves around her throat.

The Red Rose Killer?

It had been months since she'd received the red rose indicating she was a target of convicted murderer and prison escapee Boyd Sullivan.

She kicked back at the man's shins, but her soft-soled nursing shoes didn't do much damage. She used her elbows, too, but couldn't make enough impact that way, either. The attacker's fingers moved their position around her neck, as if searching for the proper pressure points.

"Why?" she asked.

"Because you're in my way…" the attacker said, his voice low and dripping with malice.

The pressure against her carotid arteries grew, making her dizzy and weak. Black spots dotted her vision.

She was going to die, and there was nothing she could do to stop it.

Her knees sagged, then she heard a man's voice. "Hey, what's going on?"

Her attacker abruptly let go just as the lights came on. She fell to the floor. The sound of pounding footsteps echoed along the corridor.

"Are you okay?" A man wearing battle-ready camo rushed over, then dropped to his knees beside her. A soft, wet, furry nose pushed against her face and a sandpapery tongue licked her cheek.

"Yes," she managed, hoping he didn't notice how badly her hands were shaking.

"Stay, Tango," the stranger ordered. He ran toward the stairwell at the end of the hall, the one that her attacker must have used to escape.

Don't miss
Battle Tested *by Laura Scott,*
available October 2018 wherever
Love Inspired® Suspense books and ebooks are sold.

www.LoveInspired.com

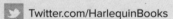